Augustus G. Cobb

Earth-Burial and Cremation

the history of earth-burial with its attendant evils, and the advantages offered by

cremation

Augustus G. Cobb

Earth-Burial and Cremation
the history of earth-burial with its attendant evils, and the advantages offered by cremation

ISBN/EAN: 9783337426774

Printed in Europe, USA, Canada, Australia, Japan

Cover: Foto ©Andreas Hilbeck / pixelio.de

More available books at **www.hansebooks.com**

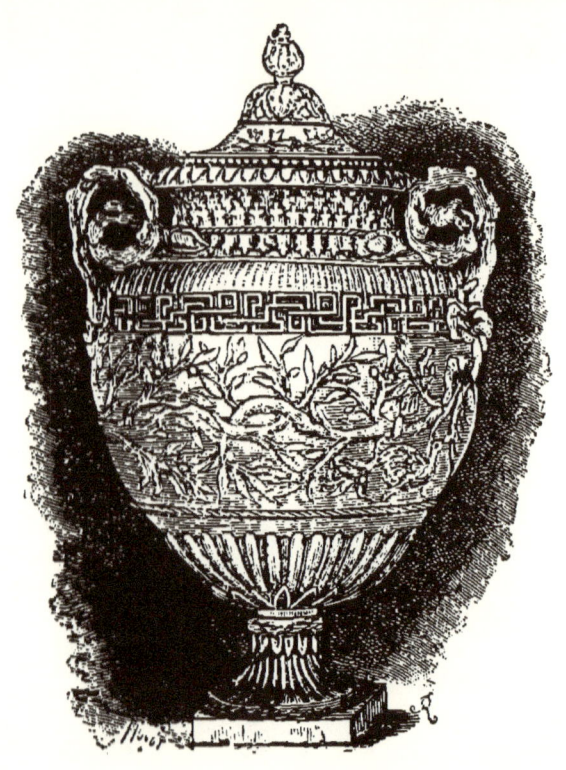

CINERARY URN FROM THE MUSEUM OF THE VATICAN.

Frontispiece.

"We believe that the horrid practice of earth-burial does more to propagate the germs of disease and death, and to spread desolation and pestilence over the human race, than do all man's ingenuity and ignorance in every other custom or habit."

From the report made to the American Medical Association, when in session in St. Louis on May 6th, 1886, by a special committee of physicians appointed the preceding year to consider the necessity for cremation.

"In the same sense in which the 'Sabbath was made for man, not man for the Sabbath,' I hold that the earth was made not for the dead, but for the living.

"No intelligent faith can suppose that any Christian doctrine is affected by the manner in which, or the time in which, this mortal body of ours crumbles into dust and sees corruption. . . . Cemeteries are becoming not only a difficulty, an expense, and an inconvenience, but an actual danger."

From an address by the late Bishop of Manchester, at the opening of the Social Science Congress at Manchester, England, October 1st, 1879.

PREFACE.

THIS little volume is written at the request of the Directors of the United States Cremation Co., who state that inquiries for a work of the kind are frequently made at the Company's office.

That cremation is steadily winning public favor is shown by the fact that in the United States seventeen crematories have already been erected, and the remains of over twenty-three hundred persons incinerated.

Most of this work has been accomplished during the last six years; and the friends of the reform, as they recall the perplexities and discouragements that attended it at the outset, may well congratulate themselves on the result.

Difficulties have been surmounted—a

good beginning has been made; and to doubt of the ultimate triumph of cremation would be a disparagement of the intelligence of the age. We do not believe that a repulsive custom like earth-burial, though deep-rooted in prejudice and shielded by conservatism, can forever bid defiance to the laws of decency and health.

In the time that is coming men will marvel at the anomaly we present in scrupulously disinfecting the homes of the plague-stricken, while their bodies are placed in the ground to contaminate the earth, the air, and the springs.

As our subject appeals with especial force to the residents of cities, whose annual armies of the dead must of necessity be disposed of in the immediate neighborhood, we have considered at length the cemeteries of New York and Brooklyn, and the dangers that threaten therefrom. If we succeed in directing on the evil but a modicum of the attention that it merits, we shall not have written in vain.

In the *North American Review* of September, 1882, was published an article by the writer in favor of cremation. The arguments then used have been strengthened, not weakened, by the intervening years: the conclusions of science have lost none of their force, and the grave none of its loathsome features. For this reason we have retained many of the arguments and examples there employed, express permission to do so having been courteously granted us by the editor and publisher of the *Review*.

AUGUSTUS G. COBB.

TARRYTOWN, NEW YORK,
April 26, 1892.

CONTENTS.

Contents.

EARTH-BURIAL AND CREMATION.

CHAPTER I.

The Reinstatement of Earth-Burial through Prejudice and Superstition.—Faith in the Power of Relics of the Dead.—Miracles Wrought at the Graves of Saints. —The Reign of Ignorance, Cruelty, and Fanaticism.

TIME and experience test the works of man, and the highway of progress is covered with the wreckage of countless inventions. The creeds, the dogmas, the social regulations of one age, may become bywords or mere curiosities for the next: but whether they stand or fall they mark the civilization of the era that fostered them; they result from conditions preceding them, while the stream of tendencies in which they are inextricably involved ultimately determines their fate.

Men do what they can, and the after generations pardon their errors, but judge their works on the merits. What is good (*i. e.*, fit), lives; what is bad (*i. e.*, unfit), dies—this is the general law. When, therefore, a custom like that of earth-burial has existed for many centuries, a strong presumption arises in its favor. Its antiquity is offered as an argument for its wisdom, and the case passes for an instance of "survival of the fittest." Let us not forget, however, that if we are to respect a custom for its antiquity, no factitious causes must have tended to prolong its life. Resting solely upon its intrinsic merits, it should challenge and survive the scrutiny of unbiased minds.

Thus judged, the antiquity of earth-burial avails it nothing, while our respect for the custom itself will lessen in proportion as we learn how it was established. A prejudice and a superstition—these were the causes, as we will hereafter show, that revived the obsolete practice of earth-burial in the earliest centuries of the Christian era. The voice of wisdom or science never

approved the use, nor was the rule of ex-
pediency allowed to test it; and thus it is
that while in legislation, science, social and
political customs and inventions mankind
has made prodigious advances, the practice
of earth-burial remains to-day with all its
hideous features, as at the dawn of a new
civilization. The cause of this anomalous
coexistence of progress with stagnation, if
sought, is easily found. With intellect
untrammelled, the children discover the errors of the fathers, and so the follies of one
century may be corrected by the wisdom
of the next; but nurtured by superstition,
an error seems capable of enduring forever.
Before eyes blinded by prejudice, the lamp
of reason burns in vain through every age;
and folly remains folly still though centuries roll by.

At the commencement of the Christian
era, cremation was the prevailing custom
of the civilized world, with the exception
of Egypt, where bodies were embalmed,
Judea, where they were buried in sepulchres, and China, where they were buried
in the earth. The Greeks, fifteen centu-

ries before Christ, invariably buried their
dead; but in time they learned the advantages of cremation, and the latter practice became universal; suicides, unteethed
children, and persons struck by lightning
alone being denied the right. The Ro-
mans, who had originally inhumed, borrowed, in turn, the sanatory practice from
the Greeks, and from the close of the Re-
public until the end of the fourth century
of our era, burning on the pyre was the
usage regarded as most honorable and appropriate. At first, it is not probable that
the funeral customs of the Christians dif-
fered in any marked respect from the customs of those who clung to the ancient
religions. The Christians interred in the
same places, and they afford us at this period a curious illustration of the blending
of the new faith with the old, by painting
and engraving upon their sepulchres in the
catacombs of Rome representations of the
heathen gods and goddesses, and even the
customary invocations of the deities of the
nether world. In time the difference became greater, and no sooner had the Chris-

tian religion become a power in the state, than its followers, always inimical to cremation, made haste to abolish the practice. They were influenced in this, not by the Scriptures, for both the Old and New Testaments are silent on the subject.

The causes, as already intimated, are found in a prejudice and a superstition. Cordially hating the old mythology, it was easy for the Christians to dislike its followers and their customs. The pagans burned their dead; and therefore the Christians stigmatized burning as a pagan custom. Being prejudiced they refused to adopt a good usage that was in vogue among their enemies; being illogical, they totally disregarded the fact that, while some heathen nations had used the torch, others had plied the spade, and therefore cremation, any more than inhumation, should not be taken for a pagan custom.

Another reason contributing to the restoration of earth-burial was the belief in the body's resurrection. That the trumpet would sound and the dead come forth was a doctrine literally accepted in a physical as well as in a spiritual sense. Again, it was part of the Christian's faith that his body was in some peculiar sense sanctified and purified: it was "a temple of the Holy Ghost." Though language like this may baffle our comprehension, yet the phrase sounded well and had due effect. The old precept of one of the Roman Twelve Tables, "Hominem mortuum in urbe ne se-pelito, neve urito," was set at naught: inanimate "temples of the Holy Ghost," by the score, were encased in the niches and corners of churches, and many a moul-dering monk unintentionally counter-bal-anced the good deeds of his life by the disease that he generated after his death.

The superstitious reverence in which the tombs of saints and their mortal remains were held enhanced likewise the predilec-tion of the faithful for inhumation. The pious Mussulman turns not to the tomb of the Prophet at Medina with greater rever-ence than did the early Christians to the grave of saint or martyr. "In the age," says Gibbon, "which followed the conver-sion of Constantine, the emperors, the consuls, and the generals of armies devoutly visited the sepulchres of a tent-maker and a fisherman. The bodies of St. Andrew, St. Luke, and St. Timothy, after reposing for three centuries in obscure graves, were transported in solemn pomp to the Church of the Apostles, which Constantine had founded on the banks of the Bosphorus.

When the relics of the prophet Samuel were carried to Constantinople, an uninter-rupted procession of devotees filled the highways from Palestine to the gates of the city.

By a heavenly vision the resting-place of the martyr Stephen was revealed to Lu-cien, a presbyter of Jerusalem. In the presence of an innumerable multitude the ground was opened by the bishop, and when the coffin was brought to light the earth trembled, and an odor as of Paradise arose, which instantly cured the various diseases of seventy-three in the vicinity. In solemn procession the remains of Stephen were transported to a church constructed in their honor on Mount Sion; "and the minute particles of those relics—a drop of blood, or the scrapings of a bone—were acknowledged in almost every province of the Roman world to possess a divine and miraculous virtue."

The grave and learned Augustine, the most profound theologian of his day, in attesting the innumerable prodigies which were performed by the relics of St. Stephen, enumerates above seventy miracles, of which three were resurrections from the dead, occurring in the space of two years. Yet he solemnly declares that he has selected only those miracles which were publicly certified by the persons who were either the objects or the spectators of the power of the martyr. Two books were published by the Bishop of Uzalis containing accounts of St. Stephen's miracles, and a Spanish or Gallic proverb has been preserved which says that " whoever pretends to have read all the miracles of St. Stephen, he lies."

Stupidity and credulity were finally carried so far that the Emperor Theodosius the First, in the year 386, issued an edict forbidding the transportation of buried corpses from one place to another, and the separating of the relics of any martyr, or the sale of the same.

The delusion, however, was universal, and not easily controllable by laws. It soon became customary to place the bones of martyrs under altars, and St. Ambrose would not consecrate a church that possessed none. Three hundred years after the enactment of the edict just cited, a council of Constantinople ordered the destruction of all altars under which were found no relics of saints. A widespread demand for the remains of holy men ensued, and "there is reason," adds the historian, "to suspect that Tours might not be the only diocese in which the bones of a malefactor were adored, instead of those of a saint."

When Constantine, the daughter of the Emperor Tiberius Constantine, begged of St. Gregory the head of St. Paul, to place in a church which she had built in honor of the apostle, the Pope (St. Gregory) sent word to the princess that the bodies of saints shone with so many miracles that even the faithful could not approach their tombs to pray without being seized with fear. In support of this statement he informed her that once when it became necessary to repair the sepulchre of St. Paul, the custodian of the place on attempting to remove some bones which were adjacent to, but did not touch the tomb of the saint, was instantly struck dead by the Ghost of the apostle, which appeared before him with terrible aspect.

The catechism of the Council of Trent approves of the custom of swearing by relics, and kings were wont to enter into compacts and to bind themselves by oath over them. These exhibitions of unquestioning and childlike faith illustrate the intellectual trend of the believing ages, and help largely to explain the preference of the Christians for earth-burial. The phantoms of the grave revealed the constitution of the invisible world, and convinced them that their religion was founded on the firm basis of fact and experience; while the mouldering bones of saints, gathered with reverent care, shielded them from accident, cured their diseases, and restored their dead to life. Well might the hearts of the faithful be drawn toward the tomb, when it yielded such precious treasures. That was the age of miracles; an age common to every race in an early stage of its intellectual development. The skeletons of saints became of priceless value, for the manifestations that were accepted as proof of their marvelous power drew, even from remote countries, riches to the churches. A universal belief in delusions like these continued unabated, through the long, profound, intellectual anæsthesia of the Middle Ages.

"In the shadows of this universal ignorance," says Mr. Hallam, "a thousand superstitions like foul animals of night were propagated and nourished. . . . It must not be supposed that these absurdities were produced as well as nourished by ignorance. In most cases they were the work of deliberate imposture." During a period of fourteen centuries thousands of instances of miracles being wrought by the relics of saints, or at the graves of the dead, were recorded and universally believed. Those with faith in the super-natural never seek after a sign and seek in vain; and miracles cease to appear only when people cease to expect them.

A collection of all the records of these alleged events published from the time of Constantine to that of the Convulsionist miracles in France in 1727, would, with the evidence substantiating them, constitute a vast library. The student of history is dumbfounded as he reads, being even less wonder-struck at the absurdities stated as facts than at the overwhelming mass of testimony brought forward in their sup-port. In despair he naturally asks himself what reliance can be placed upon the sworn statements of men in our efforts to discover the truth ? Scores of these fables are substantiated by more evidence than would be necessary to condemn a man to be hanged in a trial for murder in our criminal courts. They forcibly illustrate the unreliability of human testimony when not corroborated by extrinsic facts, and show with what qualifications evidence

frequently must be taken regarding subjects concerning which it would seem easy
to learn the truth.

What chiefly interests us, however, in
this connection, is the fact, established beyond all question, that the grave by adroit
management became a connecting link between things seen and unseen, and was the
most potent factor that the Church possessed for retaining its hold over its pros-
trate votaries. One readily understands
how the practice of inhumation was in-
sured a long life on receiving the stamp of
priestly approval. Had superstition failed
to support it, there would yet have remained the convincing argument of force.
Even before the dawn of the fifth century
the temporal power of the Church existed
in fact as well as in name, and public opinion was largely influenced by the views of
the clergy,—a body extremely jealous of
their privileges and ready to brand with
the stigma of heresy any practice or teaching believed to be even in the most remote
degree capable of impairing their dogmas
or their emoluments. As early as the year

385 A.D., at the time when the bones of St. Stephen began their wonderful work, Priscillian was condemned to death and executed as a heretic by order of the Emperor Maximus, whose action was approved by a Synod of Bishops held the same year at Treves. For fourteen hundred years afterwards the faggot, scaffold, ax, and rack were in constant use, and in order to enforce belief in dogmas and creeds which nobody understood, and to uphold doctrines abhorrent to common sense or mathematically impossible, hundreds of thousands of human victims suffered horrible torture and death.

The history of these atrocities is written in letters of blood, and they constitute foul blots on the history of man. These evils were rife during the period of Church ascendency,—" on the whole," says Mr. Lecky, " one of the most deplorable in the history of the human mind. . . . The church had crushed or silenced every opponent in christendom. It had absolute control over education in all its branches and in all its stages. . . . Every doubt was branded as a sin, and a long course of doubt must necessarily have preceded the rejection of its tenets." Mental development was arrested, and philosophy and reason, twin antidotes against superstitious credulity, for centuries were almost mute.

We are reminded of the words of Voltaire : " When once fanaticism has gangrened a brain, the malady is almost incurable." The Reformation which followed worked little change for the better as regards toleration. Neither Catholic nor Protestant had the slightest regard for religious liberty, and the eternal right of the individual to perfect freedom of thought and speech was a truth not even dreamt of. The equality of the two great faiths in this respect may be shown by the following examples :

When the noble Bruno was burned at Rome, the special charge against him was that he had taught the plurality of worlds, a doctrine repugnant to the whole tenor of the Scriptures. When John Calvin caused Servetus to be roasted to death over a slow fire at Geneva, the offence of the philoso-

pher lay in his belief that the genuine
doctrines of Christianity had been lost
even before the time of the Council of
Nicæa.

As late as the year 1748, at Orleans,
France, a man was hanged for blasphemy
and afterwards had his tongue torn out;
and in 1780, only a hundred and eleven
years ago, the Swiss Canton of Glarus followed out faithfully an injunction of the
Old Testament and burned a witch to
death.

"Heresy" was a word whose elastic
meaning embraced every opinion, every
doctrine touching belief or conduct that
could by any ingenuity be construed as
opposed to the teaching and regulations
of the Church; and the assertion of the
Bishop of Lincoln, in 1874, that a revival
of cremation would destroy belief in a
final resurrection, would, if proclaimed
from one to fourteen centuries ago, have
received universal assent.

To many it may appear that we have
wandered unnecessarily into details of
Church history, but the cause is found in

the oft-repeated statement of the anti-cre-
mationists, that earth-burial is a Christian
custom that has endured for centuries.
We cheerfully concede the point, and ask
what credit is the practice to the Church?
The general assertion, that burial is a
Christian custom, unaccompanied by facts
which qualify its value, confirms thousands
in their prejudices against cremation, and
reconciles others to a repulsive usage vio-
lative alike of the laws of health and of
the requirements of decency. Earth-burial
certainly is a Christian custom, and it has
endured for centuries; but when we consider the prejudice that gave rise to it in
Europe, the superstition that nourished,
and the intolerance that ever stood ready
to defend—when we consider these facts
in connection with the well-authenticated
cases of plague and epidemics that the
custom has occasioned,—one would think
that all branches of Christians would gladly
welcome any innovation that should prom-
ise to consign the practice to a well-deserved
oblivion. The whole question of the disposition of the dead, as the advocates of

2

incineration have again and again asserted, is a sanitary and not a religious one.

It is a question that involves no religious doctrine, and it concerns no phase of genuine Christian faith. It seems strange that in an enlightened age the cast-off emblem of mortality should be associated with a future spiritual state ; for the blending of the material with the spiritual, by merging into a heavenly body the physical attributes of an earthly one, betrays a gross conception of immortality and is worthy only of a savage race. Too often have Christians incurred this error, unmindful of the Apostle's warning, that, " Flesh and blood cannot inherit the kingdom of God ; neither doth corruption inherit incorruption."

Our sanitary welfare and our natural affections are alone involved in the final disposition of the dead, and the method that is most conducive to public health and the requirements of human love is assuredly reverential and best.

CHAPTER II.

The Conditions Surrounding Graveyards.—Physicians Favoring Cremation.—The Suburban Cemeteries on Long Island, N. Y.—Increase in the Population of New York and Brooklyn, and the Annual Number of Deaths.—Rapid and Proportionate Growth of the Cities of the Living and the Dead.—The Injuries Inflicted by Cemeteries on Newtown, L. I.—The Danger that Threatens the Springs. — The Plymouth Epidemic.—The Contamination of the Drinking-Water of Philadelphia.—Views of Physicians on these and Kindred Subjects.—Epidemics of Typhoid Fever and Diphtheria Occasioned by the Pollution of Water by Cemeteries.

On investigating the condition of graveyards, all the tender sentiments clustering around the tomb are quickly dispelled, and a state of things horrible in its nature and dangerous in its effects arrests our attention. These form the strongest arguments in favor of incineration,—arguments indeed conclusive ; and those who believe in the practice of earth-burial would seem to be

simply ignorant of the result of the custom they advocate. Scores of instances, in
cities and in rural districts, both in our
own and in foreign lands, confirm the assertion of Dr. Adams, of Massachusetts,
that "the Christian churchyard is often
a contracted plot of ground in the midst
of dwellings, literally packed with bodies
until it becomes impossible to dig a
grave without disturbing human bones;
and the earth so saturated with foul fluids,
and the emanations so noxious, as to make
each churchyard a focus of disease." Of
the one hundred and seventy-one answers
received by Dr. Adams, in reply to circu-
lars sent to the regular correspondents of
the State Board of Health of Massachusetts, both in the United States and Great
Britain, more than one third (sixty-one)
gave their testimony in favor of the adoption of cremation as a substitute for earth-
burial. And this was seventeen years ago
(1874), when the subject was first being
agitated in this country.

To-day the medical profession is practically unanimous in favor of this reform, if

on no other ground than that of public
health. At the Medical Congress in Vienna in 1887, attended by some of the most
distinguished physicians of the world,
when the question of cremation was
brought forward for discussion, there was
not a single dissenting voice: all who
spoke approved of it.

At the outset it may be well to notice a
distinction commonly made by advocates
of inhumation, whenever the dangers arising from graveyards are mentioned: they
declare that cemeteries established in country districts, for the reception of the dead
of cities, where each body is laid in a grave
by itself, are not open to the objection of
being overcrowded or dangerous. To this
we can answer that all suburban cemeteries
ultimately increase their area or become
overcrowded, while the cities for the use
of which they are intended expand in size
until in time the abodes of the living and
dead come into close contiguity. When in
1785 the horrible condition of the old
Paris cemeteries had rendered the sections
where they were located unfit for habita-

tion, the government ordered them to be
closed, and subsequently established four
new suburban burial-grounds, viz.: Père
la Chaise, Montparnasse, Montmartre, and
Vaugirard. Since these were opened they
have received in the aggregate a million
and a half of bodies. Not only are they
to-day terribly overcrowded, but by the
growth of the city they have become intra-
mural, and a report of the French Academy
of Medicine states that the putrid emanations of the first three have caused frightful diseases of the throat and lungs, to
which very many persons fall victims
every year. The conditions giving rise to
these evils exist, and are working inevita-
bly toward the same fatal end in the cemeteries that to-day receive the dead of New
York and Brooklyn. When we realize
how these cities of the living and the dead
are increasing in size and approaching each
other, additional significance is given to
facts illustrating the evils of inhumation;
and a mere glance at the condition of
things existing in this vicinity warrants

our apprehension that the public health is threatened.

At the present time, about four thousand acres of land in the immediate vicinity of New York and Brooklyn are exempt from taxation, and constitute the several cemeteries. Within them all some sixty thousand bodies are annually interred. Most of these cemeteries are organized under the act of the Legislature of the State of New York of April 27, 1847, and the amendments thereto, for the Incorporation of Rural Cemetery Associations. The greater number of them are located on Long Island, and · on the land side they almost environ the city of Brooklyn. By the aid of statistics and official data, let us consider their area and rapid growth, and the marked influence upon them of the increasing population of the two cities. A glance at the following table shows the population of New York and Brooklyn in 1890, the average death-rate per one thousand inhabitants, and the total number of deaths.

1890.	POPULA-TION.	DEATH-RATE PER 1,000 IN-HABITANTS.	TOTAL NUM-BER OF DEATHS.
New York City,	1,631,232 *	24.58	40,103
Brooklyn,	853,945 *	23.22	19,827
Population of both cities,	2,485,177	Average death-rate for both cities, 23.90	Total deaths in both cities, 59,930

On examining the above table the question at once arises as to the disposition annually made of this formidable army of the dead. Over two thirds of the number are buried in the six cemeteries mentioned in the following list. Only one of the six has been open over forty-three years, and yet within their borders are buried the

* On account of the dispute that has arisen, and the uncertainty that exists regarding the population of the two cities, it may be well to state that the figures given above for New York are according to the census of July 1, 1890, made by the Health Department, and recorded in the Bureau of Vital Statistics. The Federal census of June, 1890, placed the population at 1,513,501, and the Municipal (police) census of October, 1890, at 1,710,715. The population as given above for Brooklyn is according to the Municipal census of November, 1890 : the Federal census of June, 1890, made the population 806,343.

Since the above was written the State census of February 1892 has been taken, which places the population of New York City at 1,801,739, and that of Brooklyn at 930,633 inhabitants.

remains of over 482,000 more persons than live in Brooklyn to-day.

CEMETERIES.	OPENED.	ACRES.	BURIALS 1890.	TOTAL BURIALS.
Greenwood,	1840	474	5,713	259,893
Calvary,	1848	214*	18,487	585,000
Cypress Hills,	1848	400	2,000	130,000
Evergreens,	1851	400	6,078	115,701
Lutheran,	1852	400	8,385	208,000
Woodlawn,	1865	400	2,389	37,952
	TOTAL,	2,288	43,052	1,336,546

We have selected thoroughly representative cemeteries, containing all classes and conditions of men, from Greenwood and

* This is the number of acres in actual use for cemetery purposes, and exempt from taxation. The Calvary Corporation also owns about thirty-two acres adjacent to the cemetery, on which it at present pays taxes. These figures, together with the total number of burials in · Calvary, are obtained from Reports made to the Newtown Board of Health. From another source we learn that all the land now owned by this cemetery association amounts to three hundred acres, and that the burials up to January 1, 1891, amounted to 450,000. The New York *Sun* of December 20, 1891, in an article entitled "A Real City of the Dead," gives the estimate made six years ago by a member of the Newtown Health Board, which placed the number of interments in Calvary at that time at 485,000. The yearly number of interments since then has averaged 17,000, which would bring the total number at the present time up to 585,000, as stated.

Woodlawn, where the bodies of the rich rest under magnificent monuments, to the free section of Calvary, where over four-teen hundred of the poor received free burial in 1890. The following table shows the rapid increase in the size of the two cities, and explains how it became possible for a joint population that in 1840 numbered but 350,000 souls to supply six cemeteries, in fifty years, with over 1,336,-000 bodies.

POPULATION.	1840.	1850.	1870.	1890.
New York City,	312,710	515,547	942,292	1,631,232
Brooklyn,	36,233	96,850	396,099	853,945
Total both cities	348,943	612,397	1,338,391	2,485,177

We see from this table that the united population of the two cities is over seven times as great as it was in 1840; and its effect, in twenty years, on these six ceme-teries will be to increase by a million addi-tional bodies the 1,336,000 already received. Brooklyn is over twenty-three times as large to-day as it was fifty years ago, when the first interment was made in Greenwood;

and, as a natural consequence, this cemetery, once suburban, has become intra-
mural. It need surprise no one to learn
that its exhalations have been complained
of in South Brooklyn, and, considering the
thousands annually interred within its
grounds, and the increasing density of
population, we can readily believe that the
evil, instead of diminishing, will increase.
To support and illustrate our argument we
have cited only six cemeteries; but we
could easily extend the list. The names
of thirty additional cemeteries could be
given, located, on an average, as near
the two cities as are the six already
mentioned, and ranging from one acre
to one hundred and seventy acres in extent. In these several cemeteries, from
a few hundred to over a hundred thousand
bodies have been interred. Thus, the
Cemetery of the Holy Cross in Flatbush,
on the outskirts of Brooklyn, contains sixty
acres. It was opened in 1849, and since
1870, 109,000 interments have been made
there. This is an average of over five
thousand bodies a year; and from ninety

to ninety-five permits a week for interments in this cemetery are issued by the Health Department of Brooklyn. St. John's Cemetery, Middle Village, Newtown, Long Island, was laid out in 1882, and contains one hundred and seventy acres. Previous to being devoted to this purpose, the land was assessed at $22,000. Now it is exempt · from taxation, and during the nine years that it has been opened twenty-two hundred bodies have been buried there. Mount Olivet comprises $73\frac{64}{100}$ acres,* in which about fifty-five hundred interments have been made. In Salem Fields Cemetery, Jamaica Avenue, eleven thousand bodies have been laid away. In the Lutheran Cemetery it is estimated by the local Health Board that fifteen thousand are buried every year.

The injury inflicted by great burial-places on the neighborhood where they are located, is strikingly exemplified in the case of Newtown, Long Island. Within

---

* This is the acreage as given on a map in the County Clerk's office at Newtown. An official report that we have recently seen, states that this cemetery contains about ninety acres.

this township are twenty-two cemeteries, including four among the largest of those that we have mentioned. A map made by Surveyor Hyatt, and on file in the County Clerk's office, shows that they embrace 1,304.73 acres of land within the township. Cemeteries, however, gradually extend their area ; and a Report that has been made to the Newtown Board of Health shows that these twenty-two cemeteries now contain 1,979 acres of land, of which 1,774 acres are within the township. All of this land is by law exempt from taxation, and much of it is as desirable as neighboring farm land assessed at $150 an acre. Could it be taxed, the Report just quoted declares that a fair valuation for assessment purposes would amount to $261,650.

Thirty-five thousand of the dead of New York and Brooklyn are annually brought into this township for burial. With hardly an exception, these were in life strangers to the place, and in no way identified with its interests. They cared nothing and they did nothing for the place while living, but they become a menace and a detriment to it when dead. Within fifty years, 1,385,000 bodies have been buried in this little township,* and if existing conditions persist, less than thirty years will add to that number a million more.

Newtown has an area of 23⅜ square miles, equivalent to 14,960 acres; it contains about 17,000 inhabitants. As already said, 1,774 acres, or almost one eighth of the town, is occupied by the cemeteries, which include 205 acres more across the township lines. For every living inhabitant there are eighty dead bodies. In other words, the number of the dead buried within these cemeteries exceeds by over 46,000 the combined population, in 1870, of the cities of New York and Brooklyn.

* As this statement to many readers may seem to be an exaggeration, it is well to mention our authority for making it. A Report made to the Newtown Board of Health gives the total number of burials in the township up to January 1, 1888, as 1,245,000, and the average annual number of interments during the preceding seven years as 35,000. This average, maintained for four years more (viz., until January 1, 1892), would swell the grand total of burials to 1,385,000, as estimated above. Calvary, the oldest and most crowded of the cemeteries in Newtown, has been open only forty-four years.

These appalling facts show the grievous wrong that is constantly being inflicted upon Newtown ; and with an eloquence that needs no reinforcement, they bespeak judgment of condemnation on a community that boasts of its enlightenment, its love of justice, and its regard for sanitary laws.

The proximity of some of the cemeteries to one another is shown in the following table :

" Distance from Old Calvary to New Calvary, East, 2,080 feet ; extending both sides of two important roads.

" Mount Olivet from New Calvary, just one mile, = 5,280 feet.

" Betts Cemetery from New Calvary, ¼ of a mile, = 1,320 feet.

" Betts Cemetery from Cemetery of Device of Long Island, 1,350 feet.

" Cemetery of Device from Mount Olivet, 1,400 feet.

" Mount Olivet and Lutheran cemeteries adjoin each other.

" Lutheran from St. John's, three fourths of a mile.

" Cypress Hills from Lutheran, one half mile.

" Evergreen from Cypress Hills, one half mile."

From an elaborate Report on the cemeteries, compiled by the town officials, for submission to the State Legislature, we learn that in the old portion of Calvary about four thousand dead bodies are buried to the acre; equivalent to one dead body for every ten square feet.

One of the physicians of the Health Board of Newtown informs us that the poor who receive free burial in Calvary are interred in trenches, seven feet wide, twelve or more feet deep, and a whole cemetery block (about two hundred feet) in length; in these trenches, the coffins, with a few inches of earth between them, are closely packed in tiers. As only a small portion of a trench is open at one time, it resembles simply a deep pit about three times the width of an ordinary grave. In it the coffins are placed one above another with a thin covering of earth over them, and a portion of the pit is temporarily left open in readiness for future interments. As additional coffins fill up this vacant space, the trench is gradually extended, and the earth that is excavated on the one side serves to cover up the coffins on the other. We make mention of these facts with no intention of blaming the

authorities of Calvary, whose charity
affords free burial to hundreds of the
poor who otherwise would be buried in
Potter's Field. It is the custom of
earth-burial that we war against, a custom which, in the case of the very poor,
renders a resort to this system of
trenches inevitable.

In this connection we should state
that, in most of the large cemeteries, the
purchaser of a single grave has the right
of making in it four or five interments;
and as hundreds of these graves are dug
so closely together in rows that their
head-stones nearly touch one another,
they are almost as objectionable from a
sanitary point of view as are the trenches
that we have mentioned. In fact when
a row of these private graves has received all the bodies that are allowed to
be buried in them, the ground so occupied is in the same horrible condition as
the ground that has been used for a
trench.

An employee of Calvary Cemetery
recently assured us that the trenches for

free interments are but nine feet deep, and contain but five tiers of coffins. It is but right for us to mention this statement, although it conflicts with the following Committee report which we are tempted to present in full.

"To the Honorable Board of Health of the Town of Newtown.

"Gentlemen: The undersigned, your Committee, appointed at your meeting of January 27th, 1886, respectfully report as follows:

"That they have visited Calvary Cemetery on the 28th day of January, 1886, and in obedience with the resolutions which called for the appointment of this Committee, made an examination of the various modes of burial in said cemetery.

"Your committee first inspected the receiving vault, and found the same in good condition. From there we went to the poor or free ground. The same is located in the old Cemetery in the immediate neighborhood of the fence, which divides the Cemetery from the Road. The method of burial here is as follows:

"A trench is dug, beginning at the sidewalk, about ten feet wide and fifteen feet deep. In this the bodies are deposited one above the other, until near the surface of the ground; when a little earth is thrown over it; after this, the same process is continued one tier after another, until the plot is taken up. Consequently the open end of this trench is at no time covered, or only slightly covered if at all, until such trench is filled, when it is claimed that three to three and one half feet of earth is thrown over the whole trench, the correctness of which we were unable to ascertain, on account of the frozen ground.

"In our belief there are deposited in a trench at this Cemetery, such as was being operated upon at the time of our visit, at least 1,500 bodies in a space of 10 feet by 200; calculating that there are deposited 15 bodies in each tier, which we understand to be a fact. This method should be condemned at once.

"We then visited the new part of said Cemetery, and first inspected the ground which we understand is called the 'Temporary.' There we found about ten men shovelling dirt in a trench similar to the one above described, only deeper. The same method was here pursued, with the exception that the trench being considerably deeper, there could be more bodies crowded in a space equal to the size of the afore described. Both of the above methods your Committee considers, and is convinced, are exceedingly detrimental to public health for the following reasons. First. The trench is kept open on one side for months, allowing gases to escape from hundreds of bodies in the state of decomposition, the influence of which will extend for miles through the atmosphere, and the trench is filled with body after body regardless of the cause of death, regardless of the danger to the living in the surrounding vicinity, mindless of the still greater and more important danger to us, the citizens of our town, of polluting the water in the immediate neighborhood by the fluids of this decomposing mass entering the soil.

"Your Committee is simply 'surprised' that such inhuman methods of disposing of the dead are practiced within the limits of a civilized community, and in such close proximity to two of the largest cities in the Union.

"We also find that the authorities of Calvary make it a practice to disinter (without any permit) the bodies of children whenever an adult is to be buried in the same grave. The body is disinterred three and four hours before the arrival of the body, to be reinterred after the interment of the adult at the Cemetery, allowed to remain lying in the vicinity of the grave, surrounded by the mourners when they arrive at the grave, and in this case we also believe regardless of the cause of death.

"Considering the fact that a great many children die of contagious diseases, such as diphtheria, scarlet-fever, small-pox, etc., and considering that their coffins are often decomposed, it is in our consideration one of the duties of this Board to suppress such methods openly conducted against all rules of sanitation.

"Throughout our inspection, your Committee found a great many laws of sanitation violated, and your Committee respectfully recommends the further continuance of this Committee, or the appointment of a new one, as we believe there are other violations of sanitary rules, which require close attention from your honorable Board.

[Signed]   " EMANUEL BRANDON,
                 " F. WICKHAM, M.D.,
                      " *Committee.*"

The following Report to the Newtown Health Board corroborates what we have said regarding repeated interments being made in private graves, and quite unexpectedly affords us an insight into the

enormous profits that result from this particular method of burial.

"CALCULATION OF PROFITS OF THE CAL-
VARY CEMETERY CORPORATION UPON THE
LAND BY THE ACRE.

" Calvary's rule, which is strictly enforced, is
to make each grave two feet wide, and further
to leave not one inch of room between the
graves : the length of each grave is about seven
feet.

" Two hundred feet square ground is used
about from every acre containing 1,400 graves.
Calvary has a further custom of burying or
allowing six bodies in a grave ; consequently
when an acre is completely filled, it contains
8,400 bodies of decomposing humanity.

" The charge of Calvary for these first 1,400
interments is of our opinion $22 each, or
total $30,800
Opening these 1,400 graves five times
   at $7 each time 49,000

    Total $79,800
Cost per acre about $2,000 ; cost for
   labor opening graves, etc., at 75 cts.
   per grave : a man can open two
   graves a day—8,400 openings at
   75 cts. = $6,300. Total cost . $8,300

Profit on each acre when completely
  filled. $71,500
or a profit of 1,000 per cent.
" We are not taking into consideration the
private small 'flats' for which the Corporation
obtain fabulous prices."

This record would warrant a citizen of
Newtown who owns unproductive real
estate, in declaring that law to be a parody
on justice which taxes his land when it
produces no income, and authorizes it to
be seized and sold for arrears of taxes,
while the land of a cemetery remains exempt from taxation though yielding a net
profit of a thousand per cent. In such
legislation is fulfilled the scripture which
says, "That unto every one which hath
shall be given; and from him that hath
not, even that he hath shall be taken away
from him." It seems to us morally certain
that the Legislative Act of April 27,
1847, for the Incorporation of Rural Cemetery Associations, has been made to serve
a purpose that its framers little dreamt
of.

These two Reports to which we have

devoted especial attention are official papers, and are reproduced verbatim. They
were presented, with other documents relating to the cemeteries, to the State
Legislature during the sessions of 1888,
1889, and 1890, and were submitted for
consideration to the Senate Committee on
Public Health, and the Assembly Committee on Internal Affairs. As late as December 23, 1891, one who recently was a
member of the Health Board of Newtown
positively assured us that the charges contained in the Reports had never been re-
futed.

Against the intolerable evils that we
have mentioned the authorities of Newtown have for years contended in vain.
They see their property injured, health
threatened, and hundreds of acres stricken
from the tax-roll and dedicated to the
occupancy of the stranger dead. The
cemetery associations purchase additional
land, the supervisors of Newtown refuse
them permission to bury therein, and ultimately special legislation at Albany grants
that authority which the local officials,

supported by unanimous public opinion, have withheld. Such proceedings, by their injustice, may well arouse indignation, for the inalienable right of self-protection belongs to a community as well as to an individual; and the duty of the Legislature toward this prerogative is not to destroy it, but to defend. In the case of Newtown this right has been disregarded, and the seeds which injustice has sown, threaten to blight the town's future, and to produce a harvest of ills. It makes a great difference in this world whose ox happens to be gored. "God and the Czar live a long way off," says the Russian villager when he suffers wrongs and can find no redress; and it is hardly necessary to add in this connection that the legislators who are indifferent to the appeals of Newtown for protection do not reside in the place.

The following letter from Mr. Emanuel Brandon, a member of the Newtown Board of Health, to Mr. John Townshend, President of the U. S. Cremation Co., whose crematory is at Fresh Pond, L. I., briefly and forcibly confirms the existence of the evils that we have described.*

"WINFIELD JUNCTION, N. Y.,
March 1st, 1889.

" SIR :—

" Surrounded as I am in my township by 1,250,000 bodies of slowly decomposing humanity ; knowing as I do the bad results sanitarily, with the fact that our little township (Newtown) has almost the highest death-rate in the State, and also having opportunity to observe the method by which your company proposes to solve this 'very important question,' the disposal of the bodies of the departed ; for all these reasons I say that cremating the bodies of our dead ones is the only *humane* method of disposing of the same.

" I remain, Sir, yours respectfully,

" EMANUEL BRANDON."

Recalling the emphatic assertion of Sir Henry Thompson, Professor of Clinical Surgery in University College, London, that " no dead body is ever placed in the soil without polluting the earth, the air, and

* Mr. Brandon is the present coroner of Newtown, and to his kindness, which far exceeded the ordinary requirements of courtesy, we are indebted for many important facts relating to the cemeteries in his township.

the water above and about it," is it at all
surprising, we may ask, that, with twelve
hundred and fifty thousand bodies buried
within the township, Newtown should
have "almost the highest death-rate in the
State"? Other parts of Long Island, with
no better natural advantages than this, are
justly regarded as having a beneficial effect
upon health, and these same favorable
conditions would without doubt be enjoyed
by Newtown if the pernicious influence of
the cemeteries did not render it impossible
for them to exist.

We need not offer any apology for
devoting so much space to the consideration of these cemeteries, for a competent
acquaintance with the facts relating to
their condition gives to the arguments that
we now present a peculiar and significant
force. The total number of deaths for
New York and Brooklyn amounts, as we
have seen, to sixty thousand per year; and
allowing ten years for the complete decomposition of the body *—a process intention-

* "The estimates which have been made of the time
required for the complete destruction of a body vary
between forty and three years."—Dr. R. S. Tracy in

ally but wrongfully delayed by our present system of using double coffins,—we have in the Long Island cemeteries, constantly, some six hundred thousand human bodies in various stages of putrefactive decay, polluting the subterranean springs to an alarming extent, and giving off noxious gases and disease germs to the atmosphere. The increasing prevalence of typhoid fever in Brooklyn is regarded by the *Sanitarian* for January, 1889, as "probably due for the most part to sewage pollution of the intensest and most loathsome kind, *the seepage of graveyards.* The subsoil water of Long Island, from which the Brooklyn supply is taken, is well known to be a *moving* volume from the 'backbone' of the island toward the seashore." This process of filtration through

Ziemssen's Cyclopœdia of the Practice of Medicins, vol. xix., p. 460. Between twelve and thirty years would seem to be the average length of time necessary, according to the general opinion of those who have had favorable opportunities for judging. Each case is affected by the peculiar circumstances attending it. The disease that occasioned death ; the manner in which the body is coffined ; the nature of the soil in which it is placed ; these, and other conditions, hasten or retard decomposition.

the sand would insure the purity of the
water were it not for the numerous cemeteries and graveyards, some of them in
dangerous proximity to the reservoirs.
" Moreover," adds the *Sanitarian*, *"dangerous* proximity, in this case, consists in
the fact that the dead are placed at a depth
conveniently exposed to the subsoil water
current, carefully protected from contact
with the earth by the coffins until long after
the access of water to them ; that cases are
on record in which typhoid fever has been
traced to the seepage of sewage through
soil more than a mile in extent; the spe-
cially favorable nature of the soil and
course of the subsoil current ; and that there
are several graveyards within a quarter of a
mile of the reservoirs. Surely such conditions are alike dangerous and revolting."

Dr. John T. Nagle, Deputy Registrar of
Vital Statistics in New York City, sounded
a note of warning on this subject eight years
ago, when he declared in an interview
(*Mail and Express*, July 19, 1884) that
" the local Health Boards of Brooklyn
ought to look into the condition of their

several cemeteries at once. Such a mass of decaying humanity," said he, "if not properly buried, is very apt to cause at no distant day an epidemic of a most serious character, which if once started would sweep our seaboard." The great Ridgewood Reservoir of Brooklyn, containing one hundred and sixty-seven million gallons of water, is bounded by Macpelah and Cypress Hill cemeteries on the north, and by the Cemetery of the Evergreens on the southwest. In these cemeteries have been buried about two hundred and fifty thousand bodies. We would not have the reader infer, even by implication, that the water of this reservoir is contaminated by the cemeteries; for we have no evidence to warrant such belief. But is it safe that a reservoir should receive any portion of its supply from springs that flow through a section of country covered with cemeteries ?

"Contamination of well water," writes Dr. E. G. Ranney, Secretary of the Michigan State Medical Society, "has been directly traced to cemeteries situate more

than half a mile distant." The terrible
epidemic of typhoid fever which scourged
Plymouth, Pa., seven years ago, resulted
from the intestinal discharges of one fever
patient gaining access to the drinking-water
of the town, as the reports of the several
committees of investigation show. Out of
a population of eight thousand persons,
twelve hundred were stricken down, and
one hundred and thirty died in the course
of a few weeks. Referring to this epidemic, Dr. J. Edgar Chancellor, in an
address before the Medical Society of Vir-
ginia, at its annual meeting in 1885, said :
"If the excreta of one typhoid fever case
thrown upon the snow can infect the wells
or reservoirs of a city to this extent, what
may we not expect from the decomposition
of human bodies in the long-used burial-
grounds and cemeteries of many towns and
cities ? Gentlemen," adds the physician,
"this is no word-painting, as you know,
but solid, incontrovertible, alarming facts,
to which I beg your calm, patient consideration." Commenting on this same case, the
late Dr. William H. Coggeshall of Rich-

mond, Va., in a valuable report on "Advances in Hygiene and Public Health,"
said that "Whatever doubt could previously exist in the mind of any member
of the profession regarding the power of
previously pure running water to become
an active carrier of typhoid infective germs,
has by this epidemic been entirely dissi-
pated." And, moreover, he adds : "The
water supply of a town or city, notwithstanding the safeguards commonly thrown
around it by the municipality, can easily
be transformed, suddenly and unexpectedly
by contamination, into a poisonous condition for the uses of a community, *from a
source at once remote and individual.*"

Philadelphia, it has been stated, has a
greater mortality from typhoid fever than
any other city in the country, and the vital
statistics show that about a thousand persons die there from this disease every year.
During the first three months of this year
(1891), 910 cases were reported, of which
196 terminated fatally. The Delaware and
Schuylkill rivers are both polluted by sewage, and seven large cemeteries are drained

into the Fairmount Reservoir, which is the
proximate source of the city water supply.
When ex-Chief Engineer Ludlow plainly
told the people of Philadelphia that their
water was unfit for drinking, he was
laughed at, and the bold assertion cost him
his official head. Yet Dr. Franklin Gauntt
of Burlington, N. J., an expert on this subject, after giving much attention to the
relation existing between the city water
and typhoid, declared to a reporter of the
Philadelphia *Press*, that the Schuylkill
River, that winds through the beautiful
Fairmount Park, was positively polluted
by the soakage and drainage from the
cemeteries along the bank. We know that
about 85 per cent. of the human body is
water. "These little drops of water,
squeezed by 'Father Time' from the dead,
are loaded with sure death for the living
who drink of it. In fact," says this physician, "I have heard professional men in
Philadelphia say, that when you drink
Schuylkill water you are sampling your
grandfather. It is commonly stated that
in certain analyses made of this water

4

traces of the oil of cedar have been found, and it came from the coffins and cedar cases of those buried in Laurel Hill Cemetery." He adds : "There is another source of danger that has been overlooked. It is the Schuylkill River ice. Much of that is used in Philadelphia. People have an idea that the process of freezing would kill the germ (of typhoid), but it cannot. It is important that every drop of drinking-water should be boiled at least fifteen minutes, and after the water is boiled it must not be polluted by the use of Schuylkill ice. · No water taken from the hydrants of Philadelphia is fit to drink. Hundreds of physicians know this, and insist on having all their drinking-water carefully boiled. I have taken notice that in many hospitals this precaution is taken." In conclusion, he says : "During the last twenty-five years upwards of twenty-five thousand people have been killed off, and two hundred and fifty thousand prostrated with a lingering illness that is preventable."

We should remember in this connection that contamination of the atmosphere by typhoid-fever poison is impossible. A patient in a hospital has never been known to catch this fever from another ill with the disease. The contagion is seldom spread except by polluted water, ice, milk, or meat, bad water being the commonest cause; and because of these facts Dr. Cyrus Edson, in speaking on the subject before the New York Academy of Medicine two years and a half ago, declared that the prevalence of the disease was simply a disgrace to the century.* All physicians recognize the importance of these and kindred facts. "That the dead do kill the living," says Dr. W. H. Curtis, "is only too true; and that cholera, yellow-fever, and the whole list of zymotic and infectious diseases are capable of being transmitted through the contamination of water and air supplies is no more difficult of demonstration than it is to prove the ability of sewer gas or sewer water to propagate disease."

In this emphatic declaration Dr. Curtis is supported by that ardent cremationist,

---

* In 1891, there were 1,329 cases of typhoid fever in New York City, of which 384 resulted fatally.

Sir T. Spencer Wells, late President of the Royal College of Surgeons of England and surgeon to the Queen's household. " Decomposing human remains," writes this gentleman, "so pollute the earth, air, and water as to diminish the general health and the average duration of the life of our people"; and " existing cemeteries," he adds, " are not well fitted as safe, secure, permanent, innocuous places of repose for the remains of the dead."

The total number of deaths for the year 1891, in New York City, was 43,634; of these, 7,760, or about $17\frac{78}{100}$ per cent., resulted from zymotic diseases, a class which includes typhoid fever, small-pox, whooping-cough, typhus fever, malarial fever, diphtheria, measles, scarlet-fever, cholera, and diarrhœal diseases.* In referring to the fact that in 1884, 84,196 persons died in

---

* There is a difference of opinion among the medical authorities as to whether or not malarial fevers and diarrhœal complaints come properly under the head of zymotic diseases. We have included them among these maladies in making the above calculation, and that is the course followed by Sir Henry Thompson in giving the number of deaths caused by these diseases in England and Wales. By eliminating malarial fevers and diarrhœal complaints from the list, the number of deaths due to zymotic diseases in New York City in 1891 would be 3,988, or $9\frac{13}{100}$ per cent. of the total number of deaths.

England and Wales from zymotic diseases
alone,—a number representing about 16
per cent. of all the deaths,—Sir Henry
Thompson wrote : " It is vain to dream of
wiping out the reproach to our civilization,
which the presence and power of these
diseases in our midst assuredly constitute,
by any precaution or treatment, while ef-
fective machinery for their reproduction is
in constant daily action. . . . The proportion of deaths due to the diseases referred to is exceedingly large. And let it
never be forgotten that they form no necessary part of any heritage appertaining to
the human family. All are preventable,
all certainly destined to disappear at some
future day, when man has thoroughly made
up his mind to deal with them seriously.
. . . And one of the first steps, an ab-
solutely essential step for the attainment
of the inestimable result I have proposed,
is the cremation of each body the life of
which has been destroyed by one of these
contagious maladies. I know no other
means by which it can be ensured." *

* *Modern Cremation : Its History and Practice.* By Sir
H. Thompson, pp. 113, 114.

In 1885, as a result of protests extending over several years, by many residents of Nyack, New York, against the encroachment of the Oak Hill Cemetery upon the village, the State Board of Health ordered an inquiry to be made, and the report of its Secretary, Dr. Alfred C. Carroll, declared that the cemetery was polluting the water of the ponds and wells of the village, and its further extension was "to be deplored on sanitary grounds." In this cemetery there are over four thousand bodies buried in a space of eighteen acres, and water taken from the neighboring wells and examined by Dr. William Hailes, Jr., showed, to use his own words, "a marked degree of bacterial infection"; he pronounced it "unsafe for drinking purposes." Accompanying the reports of these physicians was that of Civil Engineer Horace Andrews, who writes: "At the present day there is, on the part of sanitary authorities, no doubt regarding the injurious effect of cemeteries upon the public health. The pollution of water is a great and manifest evil. In the case of Oak Hill Cemetery there is good reason to believe that the water in various wells in its vicinity has been brought into contact with the bodies of the dead, and holds organic impurities in solution. . . . A large part of the cemetery drainage must find its way into the neighboring ice-pond. The use of ice from the pond should certainly be confined to the refrigerating operations of brewers, or to other uses where it may be kept from actual consumption by human beings. . . . Under ordinary circumstances water contaminated with decaying substances will merely have the effect of lowering the vital powers and of increasing susceptibility to disease. But water contaminated with drainage from the bodies of the dead may be loaded with specific poison and with the germs of disease. Instances are recorded where the use of such water has occasioned frightful epidemics."

In the action of the Township of North Bergen, N. J., against the Weehawken Cemetery Association, in 1886, for the purpose of closing the cemetery on sanitary grounds and preventing further burials therein, several physicians testified to the fact that diphtheria and other infectious diseases were epidemic in the place, and that they were mainly due to the unhygienic state of the cemetery, which lies in the most densely populated part of the township. One of the physicians was of the opinion that the numerous cases of diphtheria that had appeared among the school children, were occasioned by drinking water from a well in the neighborhood of the cemetery.

Again, in the summer of 1877, when portions of the town of Hornellsville, N. Y., were scourged with diphtheria, the disease was most virulent and fatal in those districts whose wells were supplied by natural water-courses flowing from Mount Hope, where the village cemetery is located.

In 1887, when the town of Watkins, N. Y., suffered from diphtheria to such an extent that the people were almost panic-stricken, and whole families of children were swept away, it is said that the disease committed its ravages only in those portions where the drinking-water was supplied from courses having their rise on the hill west of the town. On this hill is "Lake View," the village cemetery. Thus, in both of the above towns, those who lived away from these natural water-courses on higher ground, or at more remote distances, escaped the fury of the scourge. During the alarming prevalence of typhoid fever in Carmansville, N. Y., in March, 1883, it was shown that all the cases of fever developed "on three sides of, and close to, Trinity Cemetery," and that there was no other discoverable source or cause of the epidemic. In 1884, an eminent physician of Denmark, having made a study of the cemeteries of that country, claimed to have demonstrated that ten towns have often suffered with infectious diseases propagated from burial-grounds ; and in the rural districts he says he has traced seventy-eight epidemics, mostly of typhoid fever, to the same cause.

These facts give force to the words of the late Mr. Eassie, a well known English sanitarian, who said that "the question what to do with the dead, transcends every

other sanitary problem in its importance to
the living."

It is an error, only too prevalent, to expect that water to be unwholesome should
possess a disagreeable taste. It is no more
essential than that an offensive smell is
necessary to render a neighborhood unfit
to live in. Both of these fallacies prevail
widely ; and, as regards water, we doubt if
there is a rural cemetery in this country
that has not a well somewhere among its
graves, receiving abundant patronage if it
has no offensive taste. The danger to be
apprehended from this source, or from any
streams in the vicinity of burial-grounds,
is thus forcibly pointed out by the London
Lancet:

"It is a well-ascertained fact that the surest
carrier and most fruitful *nidus* of zymotic contagion is this brilliant, enticing-looking water,
charged with the nitrates which result from
organic decomposition. What, for example,
was the history of the Broad street pump,
which proved so fatal during the cholera epidemic of 1854? Was its water foul, thick, and
stinking? Unfortunately not. It was the
purest-looking and most enticing water to be

found in the neighborhood, and people came from a distance to get it. Yet there can be no doubt that it carried cholera to many who drank it. . . . We are afraid Mr. Hadden will have to confess that at present the only known method of making organic matter certainly harmless is the process of cremation."

As to Irish churchyards, Dr. Mapother, who inspected several, declared that he "generally found them placed on the highest spot, near the most central part, whence, of course, all percolations descend into the wells."

In 1877, a malignant epidemic broke out in a section of Elsinore, Denmark, that baffled the skill of the leading physicians in their efforts to subdue it. On the drinking-water in the affected quarter being analyzed, it was found poisoned by the corruption that had drained into the wells from an adjoining cemetery. Professor Brande has given it as his opinion that the water in all superficial springs near burial-grounds is simply filtered through accumulated decomposition. Realizing the gravity of this subject, the distinguished

scientist and physician, Sir Henry Thompson, eighteen years ago, wrote, in no
uncertain terms, strong words of warning.
In an article in the *Contemporary Review* for January, 1874, urgently advocating
the substitution of cremation for earth-
burial, he declared that by selecting a portion of ground distant some five or ten
miles from any very populous neighborhood, and by sending our dead to be buried
there, we were "laying by poison, it is
certain, for our children's children, who
will find our remains polluting their water-
sources when that now distant plot is
covered, as it will be more or less closely,
by human dwellings. We cannot too soon
cease to do evil and learn to do well. Is
it not, indeed, a social sin of no small magnitude to sow the seeds of disease and
death broadcast, caring only to be certain
that they cannot do much harm to our own
generation ?"

This feeling is shared by other distinguished English writers; and the
London *Lancet* of January 11, 1879,
speaking of the necessity of devising

special measures for the disposal of the
dead, said :

" The expedient of burial in suburban cemeteries is only temporary. It may last our
time, but the next generation will be called
upon to solve the sanitary problem in a more
permanent way."

In the light of the above facts it is not
reassuring for the people of New York
to read the report of expert engineer
Charles C. Brown, a professor of Union
College, who, in his communication to the
State Board of Health, of January 26,
1889, states that eighty-three cemeteries,
providing for the dead of about twenty
thousand people, are located in and contributing to the pollution of the Croton water-
shed.

Truly said the Philadelphia *Bulletin* in
an article favoring cremation, in 1886 :

" The dead everywhere are in the way of the
living. As they lie in their graves they are
powerless for good, but they are strong for
evil. The decaying of hundreds of thousands
of victims of disease pollutes the air we breathe,
and poisons the water we drink. The germs

of diseases, such as typhoid, small-pox, diphtheria, scarlet-fever, yellow-fever, and other
maladies which often become epidemic, are
reproduced in the corpses of their buried
victims, and are sent forth to attack the living
and start new epidemics. Burial of the dead
in or near cities is thus an evil that grows at an
ever increasing rate of progression. This is a
fact recognized by men who have studied sanitary science closely, and by many Boards of
Health.''

Our cemeteries, indeed, exemplify the
law of nature that causes trees to produce
fruit after their kind. They are really
vast store-houses and nurseries of disease,
and as the magnet attracts the ore, so they,
like loadstones, draw the living to eternal
companionship with the dead :

"An Angelo for Claudio, death for death."

CHAPTER III.

THE history of graveyards in every country presents a remarkable uniformity, and
their fate seems ever the same. Under
whatever auspices they are established
they become in time terribly overcrowded
and ultimately they are closed and turned
into parks, or the grounds are sold, the
remains dug up and carted away, and rows
of buildings erected upon the site.

In our own country few are the head-
stones found that have stood one hundred

years. Prior to the establishment of suburban cemeteries some fifty years ago,
tens of thousands of the dead were buried
on Manhattan Island. Their remains, with
the tombstones on which were quaint
epitaphs that our fathers read, have been
scattered in every direction, and of all,
those only seem saved from molestation
who were buried under the very shadow
of Trinity or St. Paul's. In Paris, as a result of graves seldom being held in per-
petuity, the foundations of roads are
sometimes seen made of gravestones but
a few years old ; "and though in London,"
says the author of *God's Acre Beautiful*
"memorial stones erected to ' perpetuate '
the memory of persons, are not cleared
away as promptly, the result in the end is
very much the same." "St. George's,"
one of the London cemeteries that recently
ceased to exist, contained, early in 1891,
a handsome monument with an inscription worthy of being preserved. The
monument was erected on or about the
year 1812 to the memory of the Hon.
Noretta Pratt, a connection of the fam-

ily of the Earl of Camden, and though time had effaced portions of the inscription, yet the following lines were not obscured :

" This worthy woman believing that the vapours arising from the graves in the Church Yards of populous Cities will prove hurtful to the inhabitants, and resolving to extend to future times as far as she was able that charity and benevolence which distinguished her through life, ordered that her body should be burnt in hopes that others would follow the example, a thing too hastily censured by those who did not enquire the motive."

Her wishes, however, were disregarded; she was buried in the conventional way, and her tomb decorated with an empty urn. But time has justified her opinion, and for years interments have been discontinued in this burial-ground : since the summer of 1891 all its monuments and gravestones have been removed.

Before consoling ourselves with the thought that in our own country cemeteries are peculiarly sacred and are seldom if ever disturbed, let us recall the fate

5

of the burial-grounds of New York, and remember that in at least three of the graveyards of conservative Boston and in one at least outside the city, Dr. Oliver Wendell Holmes declares, that "the stones have been shuffled about like chessmen, and nothing short of the Day of Judgment will tell whose dust lies beneath. . . . Epitaphs," he adds, "were never famous for truth, but the old reproach of 'Here *lies*' never had such a wholesale illustration as in these outraged burial-places, where the stone does lie above and the bones do not lie beneath."

Even remote rural cemeteries, from the death of those interested in them, or from the necessity of opening new streets or constructing railways, succumb to the march of improvement. Beautiful as they sometimes seem, and harmless as the advocates of inhumation would have us believe them to be, the putrid tenants of their vaults and graves contain the germs of contagious diseases; and disinterment is always undertaken at a terrible risk.

The experiments of Prof. Tyndall and

others have shown "that certain organisms
may be boiled for hours and may be
frozen, and still survive to propagate their
species." Grain entombed with Egyptian
mummies for forty centuries has been
planted, and has sprouted into life. "By
what authority, then," asks Dr. Frederick
Peterson,* "can we affirm that life departs
from disease-germs by inhumation? How
dare we preserve vast depots in the South
of yellow-fever *fomites*, coffers of Asiatic
cholera, and every year accumulate and
treasure up small-pox, scarlet-fever, whooping-cough, diphtheria and measles?" The
sanitary records of nearly every nation
give point and force to the Doctor's questions and illustrate the danger of which he
speaks. In an address delivered before
the New York Academy of Medicine on
March 12, 1891, Dr. J. Lewis Smith
mentioned the case of an unfortunate
grave-digger, who, having disinterred the
remains of persons who had died twenty-
three years before from diphtheria, fell a

* In an article advocating Cremation, in the *Buffalo
Medical and Surgical Journal* of April, 1881.

victim soon after to the disease himself.
In 1828 Professor Bianchi demonstrated
how the fearful reappearance of the plague
at Modena was caused by excavations in
ground where, three hundred years previously, the victims of the pestilence had
been buried. Mr. Cooper in explaining
the causes of some epidemics, remarks,
that the opening of the plague burial-
grounds at Eyam, in Derbyshire, occasioned
an immediate outbreak of disease. He also
describes how the malignity of the cholera,
which scourged London in the year 1854,
was enhanced by the excavations made for
sewers in the soil where in 1665 those
dying from the plague were buried. Sir
John Simon had predicated this result, and
warned the authorities of the danger of
disturbing the spot. Sir Lyon Playfair
regards the Roman fever as resulting from
the exhalations of soil saturated with
organic remains. Mr. Eassie in his splendid
work on *The Cremation of the Dead*
tells us that in 1843, when the parish
church in Minchinhampton was rebuilding,
the soil of the burial-ground, or what was

superfluous, was disposed of for manure, and deposited in many of the neighboring gardens. As a result the town was nearly decimated ;, and the *Sanitary Record* adds, "the same would have occurred, one would imagine, even if the coffin-earth had been absent." The special investigations made by the French Government on the outbreak of the plague in Egypt in 1823, resulted in tracing the evil to the digging up of a disused burial-ground at Kelioub, a town in the vicinity of Cairo. Two thousand died in Kelioub, and the mortality in Cairo was fearful. "Even," says Mr. Eassie, "the exhalations of a single corpse buried twelve years have been known to engender a dangerous disease in a whole convent."

As high scientific authority is seldom called on to discover the origin of local diseases unless they assume a malignant or epidemic type, it is safe to believe that thousands of cases of illness and death are occasioned by the disinterment of human remains, without the true cause of the malady being suspected. When graveyards are dug up, who is there to look into the distant past and say : "This man died of small-pox, pass him by ; and that one of the cholera, disturb him not "? Remember- ing that, a few years since, the yellow-fever for two successive summers ravaged the South, how strong is the presumption that the second epidemic was largely occasioned by the burial of the victims of the first. During the state of panic that existed, men dropped like leaves, and, insecurely coffined, were hurried to common and shallow graves. Sometimes in the country districts they were buried almost where they fell. And judging the future by what has been demonstrated in the past, it seems inevita- ble that visitations of this frightful malady will yet sweep sections of the country, when infected burial-spots are disturbed by coming generations ignorant of their contents.*

* " It is impossible for any one to say how long the materies morbi may continue to live underground. Certainly, if organic matter can be boiled and frozen without losing vitality, and seeds 3,000 years old will sprout when planted, it would be hardihood to assert that the poison of cholera or small-pox, whatever it is, may not lie for many years dormant, but not dead,

In 1785, when a general disinterment
of the old burial-grounds commenced in
Paris — the work was begun in the
Cemetery of the Innocents. For years
those dwelling in its vicinity had complained of its offensiveness, and the neighborhood had become extremely unhealthy.
Although the exhumation was performed
in winter, a number of grave-diggers were
stricken with death on the spot, so poisonous were the gases generated by the buried
bodies. These foul gases emanating from
the saturated soil it had been proposed to
analyze, but the idea had to be abandoned,
for no grave-digger dared venture to assist
in its collection, knowing well, that almost
instant death resulted from its being in-
haled in undiluted form near a body.

Several instances of death from this
cause are on record. In 1744 at Mont-
pellier, France, a case occurred in which
three men died (and two others narrowly
escaped death) from entering a freshly

in the moisture and equable temperature of the grave."
—Dr. Roger S. Tracy in the *Cyclopædia of the Practice
of Medicine*, Ziemssen, vol. xix., p. 460.

dug grave in the churchyard of that city. In 1841 two grave-diggers perished in descending into a grave in St. Botolph's Churchyard, Aldgate, England. "Dr. Reed," says Mr. Eassie, "examined at Manchester some graves which had been dug some hours previously, and found that it was necessary to have recourse to mechanical or chemical ventilation before the men could descend into them. The carbonic acid gas simply flowed into these deeply dug graves from the porous surrounding soil, like so much water." "These gases," he continues, "will rise to the surface through eight or ten feet of gravel, just as coal-gas will do, and there is practically no limit to their power of escape. The danger is always persistent in the cases of dry and porous soils, exactly those which are most fitted for cemetery purposes."

The overpowering effluvia which rush from freshly opened vaults are loaded with carbonic acid and organic matter, while fungi and germs of infusoria abound. Sir Edwin Chadwick. after examining some hundreds of witnesses of every rank, was of the opinion that entombment in vaults was a more dangerous practice than interment, because of the liability of the coffins to burst.

In the light of these revelations can we wonder that the neighborhood of crowded cemeteries has been regarded as unhealthy, or that the mephitic atmosphere in which he exercises his trade, entails on the grave-digger a loss of at least one third of the natural duration of life and working ability.

All these mischiefs and dangers would be simply annihilated by the practice of cremation. In fact as Dr. R. S. Tracy tersely states (in *Ziemssen's Cyclopædia of the Practice of Medicine*, vol. xix., p. 460): "The true way of abolishing forever the *nuisance* of cemeteries is to burn the dead." The lessons taught by sanitary science should dispel senseless superstition. We know that cholera can reappear in localities where its victims have been buried, years after the original epidemic, and the same remark applies to other plagues. Well may we ask ourselves if it is not a crime against

humanity, thus to fly in the face of experience, and bury in the earth bodies infected with germs of contagious diseases,
turning the sod into a nursery and hot-bed
for the propagation of ills to curse the
generations to come. Over sewers and
above churchyards, says Sir Lyon Playfair,
bacteria "positively swarm."

Peril exists even though there be no disinterment : the infected corpse, while
hidden in the grave, can pursue its work of
harm. In a letter from Dr. Joseph Akerly,
embodied in a publication by Dr. F. D.
Allen, 1822, the belief was expressed that
Trinity Churchyard was an active cause of
the yellow-fever in New York in 1822,
aggravating the malignity of the epidemic
in its vicinity. Dr. Adams, in his elaborate
article on Cremation (*Repts. Mass. State
Board of Health*, 1875) speaking of this
locality said :

" This church was built in 1698, and the
ground had been receiving the dead for one
hundred and twenty-four years. Sometimes
bodies were buried only eighteen inches
below the surface, and it was impossible to dig

without disturbing the remains. During the Revolutionary war, this burial-ground had emitted pestilential odors, and in 1781 Hessian soldiers were employed to cover the ground with a layer of earth, two or three feet in depth. This ground was unusually offensive in 1822, and annoyed passengers on the surrounding streets, previous to the appearance of the yellow-fever in July. During the epidemic, the condition of this churchyard, and the virulence of the disease in its vicinity, called for some active measures, and on the night of September 22nd Dr. Roosa covered the ground with fifty-two casks of quick-lime, the stench being at the time so excessive as to cause several laborers to vomit. On the 25th and 26th of the month St. Paul's churchyard and the vaults of the North Dutch Church in William Street received the same treatment these being likewise very offensive and foci of epidemics."

During the epidemic in New Orleans in 1853, Dr. E. H. Burton reported that in the Fourth District the mortality was four hundred and fifty-two per thousand cases, more than double that of any other. In this district were three large cemeteries in which during the previous year more than three thousand bodies had been buried. In other districts the proximity of cemeteries seemed to aggravate the disease. Dr. Rauch personally observed, during the epidemic of cholera in Burlington, Iowa, in 1850, that the neighborhood of the city cemetery was free from the disease until about twenty interments had been made there, and then deaths began to occur, and always in the direction from the cemetery in which the wind blew. During the prevalence of the plague in 'Paris in the beginning of the eighteenth century, the disease lingered longest in the neighborhood of the Cimetière de la Trinité, and there the greatest number fell a sacrifice. In a report presented to both Houses of the British Parliament, in 1850, Dr. Sutherland testified that he had witnessed several outbreaks of cholera in the vicinity of graveyards, which left no doubt on his mind as to the connection between the disease and such local influence.

The investigations of the Massachusetts Board of Health showed that diphtheria and typhoid fever were disseminated not

only by infectious emanations from sick-
rooms, but also from the graves of persons
who had died of these complaints. And
Dr. F. Julius Le Moyne, after fifty years
of medical practice, wrote:

" The inhumation of human bodies, dead from
these infectious diseases, results in constantly
loading the atmosphere, and polluting the
waters, with not only the germs that arise
from simple putrefaction, but also with the
specific germs of the diseases from which death
resulted."

To this high-minded physician belongs
the honor of first introducing cremation in
this country. A life of observation had
convinced him that the present custom of
disposing of the dead entails pain, misery,
and death upon the living. Believing, to
quote his own words, that " men are
always bound to act in conformity to the
degree of knowledge they possess," he
built the Washington crematory in the
face of much ignorant ridicule and opposition. The future will honor the spirit
that guided him, and appreciate the wisdom that his act displayed.

Apart from the dangers arising from the interment or disinterment of those dying from contagious diseases, the cemetery possesses evils that are inherent. Dysentery, low fevers, and ulcerated sore-throats are the disorders shown to prevail in a marked degree among those dwelling in its vicinity. The air becomes vitiated and the springs and wells, as we have seen, contaminated. These are no gratuitous assertions; they are amply verified by proven facts, as we will proceed to show. But first, it may be well to recall here a remark we made when considering another branch of our subject, that these slow-paced, hidden, but ever continuing evils attract marked attention only when they occasion epidemics. Until then little effort is made to discover the source of mischief, and unaccountable cases of death are generally attributed to the mysterious dispensation of Divine Providence.

The churchyard which surrounded on three sides Haworth parsonage, weakened the constitutions and shortened the lives of the gifted Brontë sisters, whose home it was, and hardly had their achievements in the field of fiction brought them fame, when in turn they drooped and died. In the life of Charlotte Brontë, we read that "Haworth is built with an utter disregard of all sanitary conditions : the great old churchyard lies above all the houses, and it is terrible to think how the very water springs of the pumps below must be poisoned."*

The graveyard, we are informed, extends around the parsonage and garden, "on all sides but one," and "is terribly full of upright tombstones." Referring again to this subject the writer says :

"There is no doubt that the proximity of the crowded churchyard rendered the Parsonage unhealthy, and occasioned much illness to its inmates. Mr. Brontë represented the unsanitary state of Haworth pretty forcibly to the Board of Health ; and, after the requisite visits from their officers, obtained a recommendation

* This quotation and the following ones relating to the same subject are taken from the *Life of Charlotte Brontë*, by E. C. Gaskell. Two volumes, D. Appleton & Co., Publishers, New York, 1857. Vol. i., pp. 5, 38, 111 ; vol. ii., pp. 47, 48, 129, 199.

that all future interments in the churchyard should be forbidden. But he was baffled by the rate-payers . . . and thus we find that illness often assumed a low typhoid form in Haworth, and fevers of various kinds visited the place with sad frequency."

In the volumes from which we have quoted repeated instances are given of the residents of the parsonage being afflicted with fevers, sore-throats, sick-headaches, nausea, and depressed spirits; and once more the author remarks, that " the symptoms were probably aggravated, if not caused, by the immediate vicinity of the churchyard, 'paved with rain-blackened tombstones.'" Time and again Charlotte Brontë left home on account of illness, and returned with health improved, only to have her former troubles reappear. In alluding to the winter of 1852, which was passed by her at the parsonage, she wrote, " Slow fever was my continual companion." Her brilliant sisters Emily and Anne had died in 1848 and 1849—the former aged 29, and the latter aged 27 years; and in 1855, her own gentle life—a life made up

so largely of suffering and self-sacrifice—
slowly ebbed away. In the untimely deaths
of the writers of *Wuthering Heights, Agnes
Grey, Jane Eyre, Shirley,* and *Villette,* the
world paid dearly for the existence of
Haworth churchyard.

In 1740 a fatal epidemic of fever in
Dublin having been distinctly traced to
emanations from the churchyards, intra-
mural interments were prohibited. The
history of New York City, as far back as
1814, furnishes another example support-
ing our thesis. At that time, according to
Dr. F. D. Allen, who wrote in 1822, a bat-
talion of militia was stationed on a lot on
Broadway, the rear of which abutted on the
Potter's Field, from which arose an odious
effluvium. A number of soldiers were at-
tacked with diarrhœa and fever, and although they were removed at once, one died,
though the others rapidly recovered. The
Potter's Field of that day is the present
Washington Square, and years after it had
been closed to interments and turned into
a parade ground, the houses fronting on
the Square, we have been told by an old

6

physician of the city who dwelt there in
his youth, were regarded as unhealthy, and
the mortality among children living in them
was unusually great.

A case similar to the above was related
to Sir Edwin Chadwick by an English of-
ficer, who stated that while he and his command occupied as a barrack a building
overlooking a Liverpool churchyard, they
always suffered from dysentery. Instances
are very numerous of illness of this nature,
and also of throat troubles occasioned by
the inhalation of air vitiated by emanations
from graveyards. Mr. Eassie mentions the
interesting experiment of Professor Selmi,
of Mantua, who " has lately discovered, in
the stratum of air which has remained during a time of calm for a certain period over
a cemetery, organisms which considerably
vitiate the air, and are dangerous to life.
This was proved after several examinations.
When the matter in question was injected
under the skin of a pigeon, a typhus-like
ailment was induced, and death ensued on
the third day." M. Pasteur, whose re-
searches in the propagation of infection by

means of living organisms, as bacteria, have
given him a world-wide reputation, discovered that these microscopic forms of
life, developed in infinite exuberance in
dead bodies, work their way up through
the soil to the surface, there to be scattered
in every direction by the winds, with the
possibility of propagating innumerable
diseases. In Denmark a virulent cattle
disease was communicated to some cows,
from their grazing in a field, where twelve
years previously cattle dying of the same
complaint had been buried.

Long after an epizoötic of splenic fever,
a disease that annually destroys thousands
of sheep and cattle throughout Europe,
M. Pasteur, on investigating a fresh outbreak of the disease, learned that, as was
the case in Denmark, the cattle affected
were pastured in fields where previous victims of this contagion had been buried.
His examination resulted in the discovery
that the bacteria had made their way from
the buried carcasses to the surface; they
were found in swarms in the intestinal
canal of earth-worms.

The conclusions reached by Pasteur from his experiments received a startling confirmation through the investigations of Dr. Domingo Freire, of Rio Janeiro, during the epidemic of yellow-fever in that city. So important was his discovery that official reports on the subject were forwarded by the consular officers at Rio to both Houses of the British Parliament, and to the State Department at Washington. The investigations of Dr. Freire showed that the soil of the cemeteries, in which the victims of yellow-fever were buried, was positively alive with microbic organisms identical in every way with those in the blood of patients dying from the disease in the hospitals. "I gathered," says this physician, "from a foot below the surface, some of the earth overlying the remains of a person who died of the fever about a year before. On examining a small quantity with the microscope, I found myriads of microbes exactly identical with those found in the excreta of persons stricken with the disease. Many of the organisms were making spontaneous movements. These observations,

which were verified in all their details by
my assistants, show that the germs of yellow-fever perpetuate themselves in cemeteries. In fact, therefore, the cemeteries
are so many nurseries of yellow-fever, for
every year the rain washes the soil and the
fever germs, with which it is so thickly
sown, into the watercourses and distrib-
utes them over the town and neighborhood." A guinea-pig, whose blood was
shown, by examination, to be in a pure
state, was shut up in a confined space in
which was placed the earth taken from the
grave just mentioned. In five days the
animal was dead, and its blood was found
to be literally alive with the characteristic
parasite (cryptococcus), in various stages
of evolution. The injection of a gram of
blood charged with these organisms, into
the veins of a rabbit, was followed by
death in a quarter of an hour. The blood
of the rabbit was then found to contain the
cryptococcus, and the injection of a gram
of it into a guinea-pig was also followed
by death. The blood of the guinea-pig
swarmed with this microscopic parasite,

and another guinea-pig when inoculated with it died in a short time; its own blood being seen on examination to contain the same characteristic organisms in profusion. The concluding warning of the Doctor, after narrating these experiments, may well awaken reflection. "If each corpse," he says, "is the bearer of millions of millions of organisms that are specifics of ill, imagine what a cemetery must be in which new foci are forming around each body. In the silence of death these worlds of organisms, invisible to the unassisted eye, are laboring incessantly and unperceived to fill more graves with more bodies destined for their food and for the fatal perpetuation of their species."

With every contagious disease fatal to mankind, accompanying its victims to the cemetery, does not cremation become a public necessity?

Well may the *Century Magazine*, referring to this subject, express astonishment that in the face of the many and various risks involved in our modes of burying our dead, there should have been in modern times so little care and forethought. "If the breezes," it adds, "that blow from Greenwood, Mount Auburn, and Laurel Hill are laden with germs which propagate the diseases which have already slain our kindred, then the most expensive feature of those cities of the dead is not their cost-ly monuments. It is worth while to ask ourselves whether the disciples of cremation have not a truth on their side. Indeed the whole matter of our burial customs is one which urgently needs revision. . . . The dwellers in proximity to graveyards who have been poisoned by their drainage, in-clude a vast multitude whose number has never been reckoned."

These words are tame, however, when compared with those used by the Commit-tee of Physicians, appointed by the Ameri-can Medical Association to consider the question of cremation. The committee, headed by Dr. James M. Keller, in its re-port to the Association when in session in St. Louis on May 6, 1886, declared, that, "we believe the horrid practice of earth-burial does more to propagate the germs of

disease and death, and to spread desolation
and pestilence over the human race, than
do all man's ingenuity and ignorance in
every other custom or habit.   . . .   The
fatal delusion, that the earth renders harmless and innocuous the corpse, must be dispelled.   Incontrovertible proof of the fact
that the vicinity of graveyards is unhealthy is superabundant. . . .   Point to
a city, if you can, whose growth has de-
manded the removal of the dead from its
cemetery, that will not attest the truth of the
rapid production of disease and death in
all neighboring localities. 'God's acre'
must become a thing of the past.   The
graveyard must be abandoned.   The time
has come for us to face squarely the problem, how to dispose of our dead with
safety to the living.   And your committee
has an abiding faith that you will earnestly and at once say, that the 'earth was made
for the living, not for the dead,' and that
pure air, pure water, and pure soil' are abso-
lutely necessary for perfect health.   Only
skeptics deny that the dead do poison
these three essentials of human life."

CHAPTER IV.

The Revolting Features of Earth-Burial Concealed under a Mass of False Sentiment.—Instances of Burial Alive.—Condition of the Overcrowded London Cemeteries.—Some Surprising Statements by Bishop Coxe. —Description of the Process of Cremation.—Objection to Cremation on the Ground of its Destroying Evidence of Crime.—Inconsistencies Presented by Monuments in Cemeteries.—Extravagance Connected with Funerals, and the Need of Reform in the Manner of Conducting them.—The Obligation Imposed upon the Living to Respect the Last Wishes of the Dead.

WE have thus far considered the practice of earth-burial entirely from a sanitary standpoint, and the facts disclosed by such examination demonstrate the advantages of cremation.

Unpleasant truths connected with inhumation are concealed under a mass of false sentiment; and on more than one occasion when "Unveil thy bosom, faithful tomb," has been sung at funerals, we have been in the perplexed state of mind

of "Poor Joe," who, sitting on the steps
of "The Society for the Propagation of
the Gospel in Foreign Parts," wondered
what it was all about. It seems to us
impossible that a more revolting manner
of disposing of the body of a beloved
friend could be devised than by first freezing it, then encasing it in double coffins,
and burying it six feet under the sod,
knowing all the while that the grave will
soon fill with water, and that worms and
putrefaction will pursue their horrible
work for years to come. A lady, member
of the New York Cremation Society, has
informed us from her personal knowledge of
the circumstances, that, on the opening of
a grave in a Connecticut cemetery, the
coffin was found to have been transformed
into a den of black snakes, and that a number of these reptiles were killed.

A similar instance is mentioned in the
little book entitled *Cremation, by an
Eye - Witness*, viz., that when excavations
were being made in Trinity Churchyard,
New York, for the foundations of Trinity
Building, one of the graves was found to be

tenanted by a large snake, gorged with the contents of the empty coffins. No amount of sentimentality is able to neutralize in the imagination the effect of these ugly facts; and without doubt the dread of death itself is largely increased by the practice of earth-burial. " The mere cessation of existence," said John Stuart Mill, "is no evil to any one; the idea is only formidable through the illusion of the imagination, which makes one conceive one's self as if one were alive and feeling one's self dead. What is odious in death is not death itself, but the act of dying, and its lugubrious accompaniments."

If the practice of incineration were universal for fifty years, would not public opinion at the end of that time regard the suggestion of earth-burial as inhuman ? And if any one, in defiance of the general sentiment, then buried the remains of a friend, would he not be condemned for his unfeeling conduct in having consigned the body to the most revolting of fates ?

We shudder at the thought of allowing a dead body to lie upon the ground to rot, but is the actual process any the less repulsive when we have placed it in the grave under a load of earth ?

The New York *Times* of November 18, 1885, in alluding editorially to earth-burial, truly said :

" The horrors of the grave are unutterable. They are hidden by the mantle of earth. We venture to say that if the slow process of decomposition in the grave were not concealed, if it could be seen and followed by the living, the number of those who advocate the use of fire, the great purifier, would speedily and wonderfully increase."

When we free our minds from the tyranny of custom, and regard this question calmly and without prejudice, does it not seem a mockery and a sham to robe a dead friend with affectionate care, and after placing him in a receptacle of rosewood and satin, silver and plate-glass, to cover the whole with flowers and hurry him in a few hours to the fate we have spoken of? When we leave him buried in the cold, wet earth, or when we consign him to the unspeakable horror of a public charnel vault, do we not seem to have played a farce preluding a hideous tragedy?

Again, a dread of being buried alive prevails among mankind to such an extent, that hardly a discussion on the subject of burial can arise without winning favor for incineration as a method that affords an escape from this terrible fate. How frequently living persons are entombed it is of course impossible to say, as few bodies are ever disinterred before all evidence of the struggle for life would have been destroyed. But the dread of this contingency is not imaginary, as is shown by examples occasionally brought to our attention.*

The London *Lancet* of December 8, 1877, mentions a case occurring in Naples, where, on the opening of a grave shortly after burial, the desperate contortions and efforts of the victim to escape, on recover-

---

* " The distortion of features and change of posture in bodies, caused by the distending force of the gases of putrefaction, will not account for instances of bodies found inside the doors of vaults, with coffins broken open, and every indication of desperate struggles for escape." — *Ziemssen's Cyclopædia of the Practice of Medicine*, vol. xix., pp. 451, 452.

ing consciousness, had been so great as to
tear portions of the clothes from the body
and even to fracture some of the bones.
The physician who granted the death certificate and the mayor who permitted the
interment were imprisoned three months
for "involuntary manslaughter,"—but what
solace could that bring to the horrified
relatives? An instance similar to the
above was mentioned in the Elmira (N. Y.)
Gazette of April 27, 1881. A young
woman, named Mosely, was supposed to
have died suddenly in West Middlesex,
Pa. Not many days after the funeral
some friends arrived from Missouri to
remove her remains West, and on opening
the coffin, it was discovered that she had
been buried alive while in a trance, had
awakened in her grave, and turned herself
over. She was lying face downward, her
hands clenched in her hair, and her dis-
torted features plainly showing the inten-
sity of suffering she had undergone. It
was apparent that in the necessarily short
interval that ensued between her return to
consciousness and her death by suffocation,

she had comprehended her dismal situation, and turning upon her face, had endeavored to throw open the lid of the coffin, by pushing against it with her back.

The New York *Herald* of June 3, 1891, contained the following telegraphic despatch :

"ELDON, IOWA, June 2, 1891.

"When the remains of Miss Alice Woodward, at Douds, Iowa, were unearthed to-day, the young lady's body was found to be lying face down in the coffin. The appearance of the corpse clearly indicated that a terrible death-struggle had occurred in the grave. It is believed that the young lady, who was a beautiful and accomplished girl, was buried while in a trance."

How many secrets of this nature are hidden under ground will never be known; but the close resemblance of suspended animation to death warns us of the perils of hasty interment.

In the history of earth-burial are found the strong arguments in favor of cremation,—a practice certainly unworthy of respect, if it has no advantages over that of inhumation. In the words of Professor Coletti, Rector of the University of Padua:

"Man should disappear and not rot; he should no more be transformed into a mass of corruption—the source of noisome exhalations—than into a grotesque mummy, a shapeless compound of pitch, resin, and perfumes; man should become a handful of ashes and nothing more."

The advantages of cremation, and the magnitude and result of the evils of inhumation, are so well shown by Mr. W. Cave Thomas in his *Social Notes*, that we cannot forbear quoting at length from him in this connection. While describing specifically the condition of things in Great Britain, his words vividly illustrate the abominations of earth-burial wherever there is a dense population.

"Cremation," says Mr. Thomas, "insures the purity of the atmosphere and of the springs, both of which are contaminated to a frightful and incalculable extent by the present system of interment, as we shall immediately show. Data shall be given which will put the state of things resulting from this system in its most appalling light. The registered deaths in the United Kingdom for 1874 were 699,747. Taking this as an approximate annual death registry for Great Britain, and allowing ten years for the complete resolution of the body under the present mode of interment—a period, it is believed, considerably below the mark,—we have in the Kingdom nearly seven millions of dead bodies lying in various stages of decomposition, and giving off noxious exhalations by means of percolation to the atmosphere, and by sending down contaminating matter to the subterranean reservoirs. Calculating for London alone, there were, in 1872, 76,634 deaths; there are, therefore, at a rough estimate, nearly a million of human bodies festering in its immediate neighborhood. Fortunately for the springs, some of the cemeteries are on clayey soils, and bodies interred in them are, to a certain extent, locked up in their clay vaults only to be a source of mischief when they are opened. Some of these graves have been described, by one who is bound to know, as ' very cess-pools of human remains,' which give forth their noxious gases whenever broken into for the purpose of some fresh interment, as many a mourner has experienced to his cost. Bodies, on the other hand, which have been buried in sandy soils, are more quickly resolved—say in some six or seven

years.   Interments in sandy soils, however, are
more likely to endanger the health of the
living, for by percolation the fluids contaminate
the springs, and the foul gases are exhaled into
the atmosphere. . . .   It would be a good
bargain if we could obtain the adoption of
cremation at the price of double fees."

The publication, in 1839, by Mr. George
A. Walker, an English surgeon, of a volume entitled, *Gatherings from Graveyards,
Especially Those of London*, first called
the attention of the British Parliament to
the horrible condition of the city cemeteries. A committee was appointed thoroughly to investigate the subject, and in
their report, dated June 14, 1842, it was
shown that public graves were dug to
contain thirty or forty bodies, piled to
within a foot or two of the surface and
left open until full. In digging these
graves, great quantities of bones were ex-
humed, which were thrown together in a
common vault, while the soil was saturated
with putrid fluids, and exhaled the most
offensive odors. The physicians who were
examined by the committee all testified that

typhus and other fevers were especially prevalent in the vicinity of these grounds.

"In the metropolis," adds the report, "on spaces of ground which do not exceed two hundred and three acres, closely surrounded by the abodes of the living, layer upon layer, each consisting of a population numerically equivalent to a large army of twenty thousand adults, and nearly thirty thousand youths and children, is every year imperfectly interred. Within the period of the existence of the present generation, upwards of a million of the dead must have been interred in these same spaces."

It is stated by Mr. Walker, that in the course of sixteen years from ten to twelve thousand of the dead of London were buried in a plot of ground in which only about two hundred should have been laid. At the present time upwards of two thousand acres of land, valued at over $1,250,000, are devoted to the dead of the metropolis. This is equivalent to more than three square miles; and considering the density of the population in and around London, and the profitable uses to which

every acre of ground could be put, it seems
a large area of land to set apart exclusively
for the dead. Nevertheless it is inadequate to meet the requirements for which
it is consecrated. Burial acts have been
repeatedly passed by the Parliament of
Great Britain for the regulation of cemeteries, but they are evaded; and if an
attempt were made to enforce them to the
letter, probably every large city of England would be obliged by necessity to
adopt cremation. To carry out the burial
laws strictly, London alone, says Mr.
Walter Breen, would require eighty acres
of land each year to be given over to the
use of the dead. To do this is imprac-
ticable, if not impossible. As a result, in
a large cemetery near London (Ilford) the
poor are buried in trenches sixty feet long
and sixteen feet deep, in which upwards of
three hundred coffins are deposited, tier
above tier, like bricks in a wall; and yet,
says the gentleman we have just quoted,

"this putrescent mass of animal matter is not
even allowed to rot undisturbed, the companies
claiming the right of re-opening the pit in the

course of ten years and preparing it for the
reception of another mountain of coffins,—and
so this hideous process goes on from day to
day. These dreadful holes full of slowly
decaying animal matter are permitted to exist
and continue to poison the air and water, and
act as hot-beds of disease in the midst or near
great centres of population."

Realizing what earth-burial is, and what
it too often necessitates, it would seem
easy for a confirmed inhumationist to
change his belief, and agree with Dr. Anelli
that burial recalls the Middle Ages, and
even the times of barbarism, while cremation represents progress and civilization.

It must be self-evident to every rational
being that London would be the gainer if
the two thousand acres of land embraced
in its cemeteries should cease to produce
disease, and yield, instead, a portion of the
wheat which is annually imported from
America. We are reminded of the words
of the late Bishop of Manchester, who,
referring in an address to his recent conse-
cration of a cemetery, remarked : " Here

is another hundred acres of land with-
drawn from the food-producing area of this
country forever." Continuing, he said :
"I feel convinced that before long we
shall have to face this problem, 'How to
bury our dead out of our sight' more
practically and more seriously than we
have hitherto done. . . . I hold that
the earth was made not for the dead,
but for the living"; and he added:
"Cemeteries are becoming not only a difficulty, an expense, and an inconvenience,
but an actual danger."

Writers favoring earth-burial ignore facts
similar to those just stated, and indulge
either in sentiment or ridicule, like Bishop
A. Cleveland Coxe in his article in *The
Forum* of March, 1886. He tells us that
Christian civilization "substituted for the
burning of beloved bodies the gentle inhumation of the cemetery. They were laid,"
he adds, "asleep. To the secret and
decent chemistry of nature the Christian
surrendered his dead." How strangely
this language reads contrasted with som-
bre facts. Why does the Bishop not tell

us how "the gentle inhumation of the
cemetery" frequently affects the living?—
why does he not describe the manner in
which too often, as in the trenches at
Ilford, the dead are "laid asleep"? Nearly
a year before the Bishop penned those
words Sir Lyon Playfair wrote: "I have
officially inspected many churchyards, and
made reports on their state, which, even to
re-read, make me shudder."

Those who have given the subject attention are aware that for years sanitarians
and physicians, acting individually or on
committees appointed by medical associations, have repeatedly approved cremation,
after applying the skill that results from
scientific training to an investigation of the
effect of cemeteries on the public health.
Knowing this, we read with astonishment
the statement of Bishop Coxe, that "there
has been no assemblage of thinkers to give
the subject a dispassionate consideration."
The most cursory examination of the liter-
ature of cremation would have saved him
from making an assertion like this. Referring to cremation, he adds: "Those who

are the first to be ignited by a craze are known as 'cranks.'" How can this state-ment be reconciled with the fact that, twelve years before the Bishop wrote his article, some of the most distinguished phy-sicians of Italy and England were the first to organize the reform in their respective countries and were the most ardent in sup-port of it? How can it be reconciled with the fact that Sir Henry Thompson and Sir T. Spencer Wells, in their efforts to intro-duce cremation in England, were strongly supported by a petition to the Home Secre-tary signed by over a hundred members of the British Medical Association? Does Bishop Coxe mean to say that these gentle-men were affected by a " craze," and would he have us believe that he regards them as " cranks "? Is it his opinion that Sir Lyon Playfair labors under a delusion? That scientist, after making his official investiga-tions, wrote : " In most of our churchyards the dead are harming the living by destroy-ing the soil, fouling the air, contaminating water-springs, and spreading the seeds of disease."

Unfortunately for humanity, these are the words of truth and soberness,—not the words of madness. And in our own country cremation never had an earlier or a stronger champion for years than it had in one of our greatest physicians, Professor Samuel D. Gross.

Pray, does the Bishop regard him also as a " crank "?

" If more was known," wrote Professor Gross, " about the human frame while undergoing decomposition, people would turn with horror from the custom of burying their dead. If people knew what physicians know, what they have learned in the dissecting-room, they would look upon burning the human body as a beautiful art in comparison with burying it. There is something eminently repulsive to me about the idea of lying a few feet under ground for a century, or perhaps two centuries, going through the process of decomposition. When I die I want my body to be burned. Any unprejudiced mind needs but little time to reflect in forming a conclusion as to which is the better method of disposing of the body. Common-sense and reason proclaim in favor of cremation."

Thus wrote Professor Gross, who died in 1885, and whose body was incinerated at Washington, Pa. Speaking of him, Dr. Hugo Erichsen said :

" Perhaps no man ever drew breath who was better qualified to express an opinion on this subject. Who is so well entitled to form a correct opinion as the man who for nearly three quarters of a century had the closest possible relations with the dying and the dead ? "

The statements of Bishop Coxe himself stand as his most fatal accusers, for they show him strangely unfamiliar with the subject that he presumes to discuss. His account of an incineration is in itself proof that he never witnessed one. It reads like a product of the imagination, and is value-less and misleading in every essential respect. It is malicious, too, and justifies the language we have applied to it.

These strictures we do not make rashly. The writer of this volume has been associated with the cremation movement for over ten years. While President of the Company whose crematory is at Fresh Pond, Long Island, he attended over sixty incinerations ; and having personally inspected the methods employed in the crematories at Buffalo, Lancaster, Paris, and Milan, he hopes that he does not transgress the bounds of modesty in laying claim to a little practical knowledge of the subject. The Rev. John W. Chadwick, replying to the Bishop in *The Forum* for May, 1886, said :

" Those of us who believed in cremation as a wise and practical reform before we read his article, having read it carefully, believe in cremation certainly as much as ever, and perhaps a little more."

Adopting as our own Mr. Chadwick's estimate of the value of Bishop Coxe's essay, as shown in the significant sentence just quoted, let us pass to a more pleasing branch of our subject, and consider the remedy for the evils we have spoken of. By means of the modern and scientific method of cremation, the human body, within two hours, can be reduced to a few pounds of white and odorless ashes. There is nothing in the operation that can shock the feelings of the most sensitive, and the process, when thoroughly examined and understood, will be found its own best advocate.

" I have stood," says an eye-witness, " before the threshold of the crematory with a faltering heart. . . . I have trembled at the thought of using fire beside the form of one whom I had loved. But when, in obedience to his own dying request, I saw the door of the cinerator taken down, its rosy light shine forth, and his peaceful form, enrobed in white, laid there at rest amid a loveliness that was simply fascinating to the eye, and without a glimpse of flames or fire or coals or smoke, I said, and say so still, this method, beyond all methods I have seen, is the most pleasing to the senses, the most charming to the imagination, and the most grateful to the memory."

Opposition to incineration springs chiefly from ignorance of the manner in which it is effected; and to remove all misapprehension, it cannot be too distinctly stated, that the body *never* rests in flames, while during the entire process there is no fire or smoke or odor or noise to grieve in any manner the bereaved. The consuming chamber in which the body is placed is built of fire-clay and is capable of resisting the highest temperature. Under it and around it the fire circulates, but it cannot enter in.*

* This description applies to the crematory furnaces at Fresh Pond, L. I., and to others in the United States, where the flames do not enter the retort. In this and in other respects these furnaces differ from the two systems of gas furnace invented by Professors Venini and Gorini, of Italy. The gas furnaces, however, we must frankly admit, possess points decidedly in their favor, for they are heated with much less fuel and in a great deal less time than furnaces with closed retorts ; consequently they are exempt from the long-continued, terrible temperature which furnaces of the latter description are compelled to endure.

Professor Venini informed the writer in August, 1891, in Milan, that the furnace of his design in the crematory of that city, had incinerated several hundred bodies without being rebuilt, and that the necessary repairs required from year to year were trifling. The same statement was subsequently made to the writer by the engineer employed in the crematory in Père la Chaise Cemetery, Paris, concerning the furnaces of that establishment. In this crematory, one of the furnaces is on the regenerating and the other on the Gorini principle— the retort in each case admitting the flame.

Although nearly four hundred bodies are burned in these furnaces every month, a close inspection of their walls showed no traces of fissures ; and the same re-

The interior, smooth, almost polished, and white from the surrounding heat, presents an aspect of absolute, dazzling purity; and as the body is the only solid matter introduced, the product is simply the ashes of that body. During the entire process of incineration the remains are hidden from view; although in special instances, where arrangements for watching the operation have been made, no smoke, no unsightly transformations of the body were observed. The heated air soon changes it to a translucent white, and from this it crumbles into ashes. The active and consuming agent is simply air, raised to a temperature equivalent to 2,800 degrees Fahr.; and this, cooled temporarily by the inrushing current on the opening of the door of the retort, produces in the interior a most beautiful display of vibrating ruddy tints.

mark applies to the walls of the furnace in the crematory at Milan.

The two crematories in the State of New York using gas furnaces are those in the cities of Troy and Buffalo. They are according to the design of Professor Venini, and give, we are informed, entire satisfaction.

One of the first who witnessed this method of cremation said :

"As we turned away from the incinerator where we had left the body of our friend, it was pleasant to think of him still resting in its rosy light, surrounded and enveloped by what seemed to us floods of purity."

When all is over, nothing remains but a few fragments of calcined bones and delicate white ashes, perfectly pure and odorless. In all candor, is not this a more fitting destiny for the cast-off body than that it should remain for years "a mass of loathsome and death-bearing putrefaction"? By means of a Siemens furnace, Sir Henry Thompson reduced a body weighing no less than two hundred and twenty-seven pounds, to five pounds of ashes within the space of fifty-five minutes, and at a cost of less than a dollar for fuel. "After such brilliant results," says Mr. Eassie—"results at once expeditious, cleanly, and economical—well might Sir Henry Thompson challenge Mr. Holland (Medical Inspector of Burials for England and

Wales) 'to produce so fair a result from all the costly and carefully managed cemeteries in the kingdom,' and safely might he even offer him twenty years in order to elaborate the process." *

All that has been said notwithstanding, should cremation to any one still present distressing features, let him remember that neither science, philosophy, nor religion can devise a method by which an eternal parting from the form of one we have loved can be else than distressing. Let him remember that, although the thought of cremation may arouse unpleasant emotions, yet the entire process is complete within an hour, while, by burying, the revolting phases of decomposition continue for years, and may outlast a century. In the words of the great scientist, whose experiment we have related: "Each mode of burial, whether in soil, in wood, in stone, or

* " It is plain without argument that a complete destruction of the body by these modern methods is, in a sanitary point of view, far preferable to burial."—Dr. R. S. Tracy in the *Cyclopædia of the Practice of Medicine,* Ziemssen, vol. xix., p. 455.

metal, is but another contrivance to delay, but never to prevent, the inevitable change. When the body is burned, and so restored at once to its original elements, nature's work is hastened, her design anticipated, that is all." "For more than twenty years," says Dr. Parker, "I have believed that the true way of disposing of the human dead is by rapid burning—I say rapid, for chemistry teaches us that decomposition of the body, when interred, is but a slow process of combustion."

The charge that cremation would destroy evidence of guilt in cases of poisoning, is by no means as serious as at first sight might appear. By every cremation company known to us extraordinary precautions are taken to obviate this danger, as appears from the rules relating to the subject laid down by the managers of the crematory at Fresh Pond, Long Island; and these are essentially the same as those followed by other companies throughout the country. An application for incineration at Fresh Pond must be made by the person having charge of the disposal of the body, or

his representative, and a printed list of
questions in blank, prepared by the company, must be filled out and signed by
such person and filed in the company's
office. An original certificate from the
physician who attended the deceased, stating time, place, and cause of death, must
also be presented before an order directing
the incineration will be granted to the applicant. Upon the arrival of the remains
at the crematory, a burial permit issued
by the Board of Health, the physician's
certificate already referred to, and the
order authorizing the incineration by the
company must be delivered to the superintendent; and the rule is absolute that unless these three papers are complete in
every respect and duly presented, the incineration under no circumstances will be
allowed to take place. We should remember that suspicious circumstances warrant-
ing official investigation are almost invariably observed before or about the time of
death, and if a coroner's jury is not impaneled before a burial, the chances are very
small that one will be impaneled afterward.

Besides, in the few instances where bodies are disinterred for post-mortem investigations, it is almost certain that enough was previously known or suspected to have prevented such bodies from being incinerated. Under suspicious circumstances, or pending the settlement of disputes, bodies are sometimes buried, as it is known that if necessary they can be disinterred; but in such cases incineration would, as a precaution, be forbidden.* Not one body in a million, according to the statement of a chemist to Dr. Peterson, is disinterred to be examined for suspected poisoning; still in case of incineration mineral poisons could be discovered in the ashes, or sublimated in the gases, while, with the exception of the one alkaloid strychnia (we quote

* At the suggestion of Sir Henry Thompson a careful and systematic inquiry was made throughout England and Wales to ascertain the number of exhumations for the last twenty years. From the data obtained we learn that the average number of exhumations made in a year is only five, and less than one yearly for poison. We recognize the full significance of this statement on learning that the total number of deaths in England and Wales during the year 1886 was 537,276.—*Modern Cremation*, pp. 114, 118, 119.

from Dr. Peterson), all vegetable poisons—
those most to be dreaded—decompose
with the body, and therefore as to these
the result will be the same whether the
body be burned or buried.

Regarded from the artist's point of view,
our attractive cemeteries, notwithstanding
their picturesque effects, present strange
inconsistencies; while our climate prevents
a display of the finest and most delicate
art, and, in fact, renders them for almost
six months of the year unfit to be visited.
The magnificent and ponderous mausoleum
within which the Roman or the Greek
would have deposited, secure from molestation, the cinerary urns of his ancestors,
is planted by us directly above some la-
mented progenitor, as if to deprive him of
the privilege of the resurrection.   On
every hand marble urns destitute of ashes
crown lofty columns, and inverted torches,
typical of cremation, meet the eye.   These
are the borrowed tokens of a classic age,
that in our modern cemeteries lose their
ancient meaning, and serve no obvious
purpose.   Another charge that can be

brought against cemeteries, is the expenditure in them annually of enormous sums of money, sums entirely disproportionate to the services they yield. In an address to the Chicago Medical Society, in advocacy of cremation, Dr. Charles W. Purdy made some striking comparisons to show what a burden is laid upon society by the burial of the dead. According to his carefully prepared estimate, " one and one fourth times more money is expended annually in funerals in the United States than the Government expends for public school purposes. Funerals cost this country in 1880 enough money to pay the liabilities of all the commercial failures in the United States during the same year, and give each bankrupt a capital of eight thousand six hundred and thirty dollars with which to resume business. Funerals cost annually more money than the value of the combined gold and silver yield of the United States in the year 1880." These figures, incredible as they appear, do not include the enormous sums invested in burial-grounds and expended in tombs and monuments, nor the loss from depreciation of property in the vicinity of cemeteries.

As a return for this unparalleled and ridiculous extravagance, we have the funeral, the most doleful and melancholy function on earth, and the ordinary graveyard, transitory and repulsive in its nature, and deadly in its effect. When, in addition to these facts, we remember that, notwithstanding the vast sums expended, each semblance of poor humanity has been screwed up in a box for a decay as odious as it is needless, we find it easy to agree with the author of *God's Acre Beautiful* who declared the burial system in vogue to be "the most impudent of the ghouls that haunt the path of progress."

The money lavished by the citizens of New York during the past ten years on funerals and cemeteries would have supplied a temple for the ashes of the dead in every way worthy of the metropolis. Added to and embellished by coming generations, its halls of statuary would foster art and rob Death of half his terror. There, cin-

erary urns of every design and every degree of elegance could be placed, safe from
all desecration. Money expended upon
them would be better employed than by
being spent on coffins, which, within a few
hours, are buried forever from sight; while,
from a sentimental point of view, it would
appear less incongruous to dress with roses
a beautiful bronze or silver vase containing the ashes of a friend, than to tie a
wreath of immortelles to the door-knob of
a gloomy vault.

Another subject well merits attention
here—the manner of conducting funerals.
A funeral would seem to be essentially a
family matter, and because of the circumstances surrounding it, simplicity and privacy should prevail. In the hour of bereave-
ment when the grief-stricken family are to
part with their dead, how heartless and
how senseless is that custom which necessitates public obsequies or calls for any display. It is heartless, because it adds to the
grief of the mourners. Then, if never before,
they seek to avoid publicity, for the side-
long glance of curiosity at such time is not

pleasant to meet. It is senseless, because it serves no worthy purpose. Flattery cannot soothe the ear of death, and a funeral conducted in public with all the pomp that wealth and vanity can devise, adds nothing to the esteem in which one's memory is held. One kindly act in life outlasts it all. Sincere grief is retiring, and is not to be comforted by show. It is a good omen therefore for decency and public policy that people of refinement are already beginning to set an example in this respect. We all know that vulgar ostentation at funerals in the past has had upon the poor a most pernicious effect. Too often in such cases when death ends a protracted illness with all its attendant and unavoidable expense, at the very hour when economy should commence, extravagance unfortunately begins. Who has not seen enough money spent on carriages and "floral emblems" to support the dead man's helpless children many months? Who has not known of families being deprived of necessities because of these follies, and the bills in the end paid by means of a subscription paper? Watch

certain funerals as they pass you daily in
the streets. You will see grown men in
the carriages laughing and smoking cigars,
and children eating cake. In Heaven's
name where, in such an exhibition, can you
find the element of respect? Unfortunately,
those who encourage this foolishness are not
the ones to suffer from it.

Our funeral customs need reforming, for
some of them seem barbarous : they arm
with new terrors, death. Taking a dead
person from his home to a church, and ex-
posing him there to the public gaze, appears
to us unnecessary and in bad taste. Famili-
arity with the sight does not reconcile us
to it. It is cruel to the mourners. They
sit in the front pews with stricken hearts,
the martyrs to unfeeling custom. They hear
the doleful hymns, and the long prayers and
sermons, with their platitudes on *resigna-
tion;* all useless in such an hour. A state
of subdued excitement exists ; the very air
is oppressive. Persons barely acquainted
with the deceased in life feel privileged to
be present. They pass conflicting com-
ments on the appearance of the corpse, or

watch with morbid curiosity the last acts at the open grave. Cremation presents no heart-rending scene like this. Who having heard it can forget the harsh grating of the ropes as they are drawn from under the coffin ; or the thud of the earth as it is shoveled down upon the lid. And thus the buried form is abandoned to its fate, and a harrowing and uncalled for public spectacle comes to an end. Truly human ingenuity has woven a tissue of horrors to be dropped as a curtain at the close of a human life. Death in itself is solemn and impressive, but it gains nothing in impressiveness by a ceremony like this.

Let us hope that the day is not distant when our funerals will be conducted more privately than at present, and be free from all inconsistencies. The social amenities of life require us in daily intercourse with our friends outwardly to respect their views although we may not accept them. May love and fidelity strengthen that respect when their eyes are closed and their voices are silent.

We should have no services over them

*that they did not approve of while living;
nor should we dispose of their bodies in a
manner that violates their requests.* The
most sincere tribute to the memory of our
dead consists in obedience to their wishes.
And if any particular funeral service conflicting with the deceased one's views
would afford consolation to the mourners,
could they not with propriety deny themselves such comfort until after the body is
removed to its last destination?

Fidelity in death is the strongest evidence of affection, and instances of it in
any age command the deepest respect.
When pursued by adversity, the great
Pompey fled from Pharsalus to Egypt; he
was basely betrayed and assassinated and
his headless body left upon the sea-shore.
A faithful freedman who had clung to him
through all adversities alone remained to
mourn. Gathering a quantity of wood, he
burned the remains and carefully collected
the ashes. And thus from the hands of a
single humble friend the once mighty ruler
of Rome received the last tribute of respect
and love. The sincerity of affection prompt-

ing this pious act touches our generous feelings, and as an example of simple devotion, steadfast in misfortune and death, it arouses our sympathy far more than does the " mouth honor," pomp, and freezing solemnity of the conventional public funeral.

CHAPTER V.

The Progress of Cremation.—Revival of Interest in the Subject in Italy and other Countries of Europe.—Distinguished Men Advocating its Introduction.—Petition to the German Reichstag.—Cremation in Japan.—Advance of the Movement in the United States.—Crematories and Societies in Existence in Different Cities of the Union.—Friendly Aid of Medical Associations. — Legislative Action Favoring the Reform. — The Crematory at Quarantine Station, New York. — Other Establishments.—Work of Dr. Davis and Dr. Erichsen.—Prejudice against Cremation Dispelled by Witnessing the Process.—The Professions Represented by those who have been Incinerated.—Bright Prospects for the Future.

As the evils incidental to earth-burial will be abolished when the system giving rise to them is supplanted by cremation, the advance of the latter reform in popular regard becomes a matter of unusual importance. Let us consider, therefore, the progress that it has made, both in Europe and in this country, during the years that have elapsed since interest in the subject was re-awakened in Italy. In 1869 Professors Coletti and Castiglioni, " in the name of public health and of civilization," introduced in the Medical International Congress at Florence the question of cremation. At that time not a single crematory had as yet been built either in Europe or America. A resolution was passed at this Congress urging that every possible means be employed to promote the substitution of incineration for burial; and, three years later, the Royal Institute of Science and Letters of Lombardy, offered a prize for the best practical method. From this time forward interest in the movement steadily increased, and cremation found indefatigable champions among some of the most learned professors and physicians of Italy. The work of Dr. Gætano Pini and Professors Coletti and Castiglioni in that country was ably seconded by the efforts of Sir Henry Thompson, Sir T. Spencer Wells, and the late Mr. William Eassie in England. Sir Henry Thompson was President of "The Cremation Society

of England," founded in January, 1874; and
two articles by him relating to the treatment of the body after death, and strongly
advocating the adoption of cremation, appeared in the *Contemporary Review* for
January and March of that year, and at-
tracted unusual attention throughout England and in this country. Mr. William
Eassie, the eminent sanitary engineer, was
Secretary of this Society, and in December,
1874, published a book entitled *Cremation
of the Dead; Its History and Bearings
upon Public Health.* This masterly work
gained great celebrity, and will always
remain a standard authority upon the
subject.

In August, 1880, Sir T. Spencer Wells
read an able paper, advocating cremation,
before the British Medical Association at
Cambridge; and a memorial indorsing the
adoption of incineration was subsequently
drawn up and signed by over a hundred
prominent physicians and surgeons, members of the Association. It was addressed
and forwarded to the Home Secretary, and
stated that the signers were opposed to the

existing custom of burying the dead, and desired to substitute in place of it cremation. As the latter practice was not illegal, they trusted that the government would interpose no obstacles to its introduction. While the advocates of cremation were thus employed in England, in our own country Dr. F. Julius LeMoyne, Prof. Samuel D. Gross, and other physicians were ably and earnestly laboring to promote the reform here. The result of these and other efforts, made at the same time in Germany, France, Switzerland, and Denmark was quickly felt, and by 1876 the merits of the question were under discussion in nearly every country of the civilized world.

But periods of long and earnest weighing of the opposing opinions invariably precede any innovations upon old customs, and cremation furnished no exception to the rule. As late as 1881, only eleven years ago, Europe and America together possessed but five crematories. Of these, two were in Italy, at Milan and at Lodi, and were erected in 1874 and in 1876. A third was at Washington, Pa. It was built by

Dr. F. Julius LeMoyne, and the first in-cineration performed there was that of the Baron de Palm, in December, 1876. A fourth crematory was at Gotha, Germany. It was built by the Municipal Council of that city, and was opened to the public in November, 1878. The fifth was at Woking, Surrey, England. This crematory was built in 1879 ; in it the system invented by Pro-fessor Gorini, of Italy, was adopted. It took six years, however, in England to dis-cover that there was no law, ancient or modern, forbidding the practice of crema-tion, provided it be done so as to cause no nuisance. As a result of this delay no incineration took place at Woking before March 26, 1885. The first four cremato-ries, however, had, by 1881, presented to the world over two hundred successful and practical tests of incineration, and public interest in the movement had become wide-spread. In nearly all the great cities of our own country and of Europe, cremation societies had been thoroughly organized, and to-day their membership rolls contain in the aggregate the names of thousands of persons. Distinguished scientists and physicians in every country heartily indorsed the movement, and men illustrious in other walks of life added their support. In Denmark, Bishop Mourad, who, during the war with Prussia, led the affairs of the nation as prime-minister, publicly declared himself in favor of a law that would compel the substitution of cremation for earthburial. Lord Beaconsfield, in considering earth-burial, wrote : " What is called God's acre is really not adapted to the country which we inhabit, the times in which we live, and the spirit of the age." Gambetta was a member of the French Cremation Society, and General Garibaldi in his will explicitly directed that his body should be burned, and that the urn containing his ashes should be placed under the orange tree shading the tombs of his two little girls.

Under such favorable auspices it is not surprising that during the last ten years cremation has advanced with rapid strides. In 1888 it was stated, at a Congress of Cremation Societies in Vienna, that there were fifty crematories in the world. Of these, twenty were located in the cities and towns of Italy, and the rest were scattered throughout the United States and in different countries of Europe. Lodi, Cremona, Brescia, Padua, Milan, Varese, Florence, Venice, Rome, London, Paris, Copenhagen, Stockholm, Gothenburg, Gotha, Dresden, and Brussels were some of the cities of Europe that in 1888 possessed crematories, while almost every town of any importance had already organized a cremation society. During the ten years following the revival of cremation in Italy, from April, 1876, to December 31, 1886, 787 incinerations took place in that country alone, and the crematory at Gotha, eight years after being built, had incinerated over five hundred bodies.

As cremation societies were multiplied in Germany, Prince Bismarck declared that he had no objection to the enactment of a general law regulating and permitting the practice of cremation throughout the entire empire; removing thereby the restriction that had previously confined the right to

Gotha. Encouraged by this token of official favor, toward the close of the year 1885 the friends of cremation laid before the Reichstag a petition, containing 23,365 signatures, earnestly requesting that the practice of incineration be allowed in all the cities of Germany. The following account of the professions of the subscribers shows in what quarters cremation found most favor : The list was signed by 1,942 physicians; 1,046 lawyers and professors; 849 school teachers ; 1,015 government officers ; 10 Protestant clergymen; 3 rabbis; 361 women ; and 6,000 workingmen; the remaining number being made up of merchants, manufacturers, tradesmen, and others. The Berlin Society now has over a thousand members, and the chief publication in the interest of cremation, *Die Flamme,* is issued monthly in that city. The December number of 1891 completed a list of 2,188 incinerations that had taken place in different parts of the world, and accounts of which had been forwarded for publication. The list necessarily is far from complete, as many cremations take place that are never announced to the Berlin journal.

The Cremation Society of France, founded in 1880, has a membership of about six hundred persons. In 1886 the Municipal Council of Paris suggested to the Prefect of Police that the remains of some four thousand persons annually dissected in the hospitals should be cremated, in order to relieve the overcrowded cemeteries and for the sake of economy. The suggestion was approved of, and the Prefect of the Seine decided that the crematory should be erected in the cemetery of Père la Chaise. This has been done, and the building, a handsome and commodious one, is now open for public use. It cost, with its two furnaces, about $50,000 ; and, as already stated, one of these is a Gorini, the other, a regenerating furnace. Together, they are estimated to be able to cremate five thousand bodies annually. The first incineration took place on the 22d of October, 1887, and since then nearly four thousand bodies have been consumed.

In Portugal, organized and violent opposition was shown on the part of the clergy to the introduction of incineration; but the teachings of science prevailed in the end, as they generally do, and to-day the use of cremation is not only optional throughout the kingdom, but the authorities of Lisbon have decreed that it shall be compulsory in time of epidemics. In 1885, it might be added, the Italian government built a crematory for the cholera hospital at Varignano. The Swiss Society at Zurich has a membership of 400, and the Society of Holland, with branch societies in ten different parts of the kingdom, numbers 1,500 members. The Brussels Society, founded in 1882, counts over 600 members; while the Danish Society at Copenhagen, organized in 1881, has over 1,800 members, of whom 120 are physicians.

Cremation has likewise made great progress in Japan. In Tokio alone there are six crematories open to the public, and about 10,000 bodies a year are burnt in that city. Most of the crematories throughout the country are owned by stock companies, though some wealthy families have private ones. It is estimated that about forty-seven per cent. of all the dead in Japan are incinerated.

Let us turn now to the condition of cremation in the United States, and see if it offers encouragement to its advocates. Between 1881 and 1885 a number of cremation societies were organized in different cities of the United States, and many lectures were delivered, and pamphlets and articles published advocating the reform. Efforts made during preceding years to attract attention to the work had met with but little success, and it was only during the years above specified that a general popular interest became manifest. The work done by the different societies during these years was almost entirely educational. The object of all of them was about the same. As expressed in the by-laws of the New York Cremation Society, it was "to disseminate sound and enlightened views respecting the incineration of the dead; to advocate and promote, in every proper and legitimate way, the substitution of this method for burial; and to advance the

public good by affording facilities for car-
rying cremation into operation." The
steady, unobtrusive work of these societies
was destined ultimately to produce good
results, although as late as the spring of
1884, only eight years ago, there was but
one crematory in the entire country. This
is an important fact in view of what follows, and should not be forgotten. The
crematory in question was that erected by
Dr. F. Julius LeMoyne at Washington,
Pa., and first used, as already stated, at the
incineration of the Baron de Palm in December, 1876.

Within two years after it was opened
over sixty applications for prospective cremations were made, but declined, for the
reason that the crematory was built for
private use, and not for the purpose of
continuing a regular business. An occa-
sional cremation was permitted, only with
the object of keeping the subject before
the public eye. After thirty-eight or forty
incinerations had taken place, the building
on the 1st of August, 1884, was closed to
the general public.

On November 25, 1884, the second crematory ever built in this country was opened at Lancaster, Pa. It was erected by a number of public-spirited citizens of the place, and the furnaces were designed and built by Dr. M. L. Davis, of Lancaster, a gentleman whose untiring energy in promoting the advance of the reform has caused his name to be known and respected in every cremation society throughout the land. Early in December, 1885, the beautiful Buffalo crematory, and the crematory of the United States Cremation Co., located at Fresh Pond, Long Island, had their first incinerations. From this time forward the movement showed steady progression, and new crematories were opened every year. In 1888 there were eleven crematories in the country; and this number at the opening of 1891 had increased to seventeen. Fifteen out of the seventeen have been built during the last six years. They are located in the following places, the list being given in the order in which the buildings were opened : Washington, Pa.; Lancaster, Pa.; Buffalo, N. Y.; Fresh Pond,

Long Island; Pittsburg, Pa.; Med. Dep't,
University of Pennsylvania; Los Angeles,
Cal.; Cincinnati, O.; Detroit, Mich.; St.
Louis, Mo.; Germantown, Pa.; Quarantine
Station, N. Y.; Baltimore, Md.; Troy, N.Y.;
Philadelphia, Pa. (City Burial Ground);
Atlanta, Ga.; Davenport, Ia. The reports made by the officers of these several
crematories show that the remains of
about 2,200 persons in all had been incinerated by the beginning of May, 1891.
This we consider a remarkably good showing for a country that had but one crematory within its borders only seven years
before. Other crematories are about to be
erected in Boston, Mass.; Chicago, Ill.; San
Antonio, Tex.; and at Des Moines, Ia.
During the past ten years as many as
twenty-two cremation societies were organized and are now in existence in different
cities of this country. In their efforts to
popularize and extend the reform they have
been encouraged by the friendly aid of
medical associations, and at times benefited
by legislative action. In September, 1883,
the Grand Jury of New Orleans recom-

mended that, on sanitary grounds, a crematory should be established in that city, for
burning the bodies of those who die of
contagious diseases. In May, 1885, the
Legislature of Massachusetts passed an act
authorizing the formation of corporations
for the purpose of cremating the bodies of
the dead.

In June, 1886, a committee on cremation
appointed by the "Society of Medical
Jurisprudence and State Medicine" of
New York City, made a report recommending in strong language this method of disposing of the dead. It declared cremation
to be a sanitary necessity, and advised its
acceptance by all. Accompanying the report was a resolution recommending the
passage of a bill by the Legislature that
would require all persons who die of contagious diseases, like small-pox, cholera, and
yellow-fever, to be cremated under the direction of the municipal authorities. The
bill was to provide also for the cremation
of the bodies of paupers, and persons of
unknown identity. Public crematories
were deemed advisable and recommended.

Of all the physicians present at the time of the submission of this report, only two expressed opinions unfavorable to it. New York was the first State to order by Legislative action, the erection of a crematory, and to set apart money for that purpose. The Legislature of 1888 appropriated $20,000 for the building and equipping of a crematory on Swinburne Island for the use of the Commissioners of Quarantine, and for the removal and disposition of the bodies formerly buried at Seguine's Point, the burying-ground of the establishment. The crematory was built in 1888 by Dr. M. L. Davis of Lancaster, Pa., at a cost of $5,500. A mortuary was also erected on the Island, with a capacity for thirty-two bodies, to receive temporarily the remains of those who die at the Quarantine hospital, or whose religious views as communicated by them while living, or by their friends within twenty-four hours after their decease, are opposed to cremation. The section of the act directing the removal of the dead from Quarantine cemetery (Seguine's Point), provided that the bodies should be " dis

posed of in such manner as will not endanger the public health." In conformity with
this order the remains of nearly three hundred persons were disinterred and incinerated at the crematory, and the ashes
collected and deposited in the mortuary
already mentioned. During 1889 and 1890
the bodies of eight persons who died at
the Quarantine hospital were also incinerated. The establishment of this crematory,
we are informed, gives great satisfaction to
the Health Officers, and successfully solves
a problem that presented at times in the
past serious difficulties.

In 1886 the University of Pennsylvania
erected a crematory for the incineration of
the remains of those dissected in the Medical Department of the University ; and in
1890, by the municipal authorities of Philadelphia, a crematory was erected on the
public burial-ground of that city. Both of
these crematories were built by Dr. M. L.
Davis ; and it may be mentioned in this
connection that nine crematories in different States have had their furnaces built
under the direct superintendence and ac-

cording to the plans designed by this physician.

He also founded *The Modern Crematist*
at Lancaster, a monthly journal published
in the interest of the reform, and giving an
account of its progress, both in this country
and in Europe.   The devotion of this
physician to the cause is typical of the at-
titude of the entire medical profession.   In
our own country, the four physicians most
prominently identified with the work were
Dr. LeMoyne, Prof. Gross, Dr. Davis, and
Dr. Hugo Erichsen.   The last gentleman
was a regular contributor to *The Crematist*, and in 1887 he published a valuable
book of over two hundred and fifty pages
on the " Cremation of the Dead."   It was
largely as a result of his personal efforts
that in 1887 a crematory was built in
Detroit, his place of residence.   To both
Dr. Davis and Dr. Erichsen we would
cheerfully acknowledge our indebtedness,
for their writings have furnished us with
many valuable and important facts relating
to our subject.

Some of the crematories that we have

mentioned are richly decorated, and possess architectural beauties worthy of notice. The one at Buffalo is built of dark-brown sandstone: it is a substantial structure, and with its square tower and steep slanting roof resembles some of the chapels built in the north of England centuries ago. The building is covered with ivy, and surrounded by sloping lawns. The interior resembles a chapel, and the chancel and nave are beautifully decorated in early Italian style. It has windows of richly stained glass, and some twenty different symbols and devices are interwoven in arches of green and blue. All the surroundings combine to show both respect for the dead and respect for the feelings of the living.

The crematory in Oakwood Cemetery, Troy, N. Y., was completed in November, 1889, and is one of the finest buildings of its kind in the world. It is an imposing and costly structure, built of Westerly granite, in Romanesque style, and was erected by Mr. and Mrs. William S. Earl as a memorial to their son, the late Gardiner Earl. The building is 136 feet long, 70 feet wide, and has a tower 90 feet in height. Wealth and affection combined have succeeded in making this crematory a model for future societies to study. After personally examining the different systems of incineration in use, Mr. Earl decided that the Venini method was the one best adapted for the purpose, and it was accordingly introduced in the memorial crematory. This is the system of incineration employed at the Buffalo Crematory (New York), the one at Milan, and other leading establishments of Italy. The temple of the Philadelphia Cremation Society is another beautiful structure, erected on the grounds of the Chelten Hills Cemetery at Germantown. It contains a chapel with a seating capacity of three hundred persons, and also an extensive columbarium, with niches for receiving the urns that preserve the ashes of the dead.

We may appropriately refer to the effect produced on persons when they first witness an incineration, for the impressions made at such a time influence the growth of the reform. While the writer was in correspondence with officers of different societies, during the preparation of this volume, no information was more welcome or encouraging than that so frequently received, of persons coming to witness incinerations with aversion and prejudice and subsequently going away well pleased. It conforms with our 'personal experience at the Fresh Pond Crematory on Long Island, where hardly an incineration took place without some one voluntarily confessing that, having witnessed the process, a previous unfavorable opinion regarding it was dispelled. We know of many incinerations that have occurred as a direct result of the satisfaction afforded by other incinerations preceding them. A steady, natural growth from such a cause is in the highest degree satisfactory. It clearly indicates that the process is approved of, and that its popularity is destined to increase and be lasting. At the Fresh Pond Crematory incinerations are always as private as the relatives of the deceased may desire. The audience room belongs to them for the time being, and their wishes as regards the exclusion or admission of visitors are strictly observed. When they do not require strict privacy, orderly persons are allowed to be present; and when incinerations are not in progress visitors are always admitted, and the method employed thoroughly and patiently explained. This course of procedure tends to make friends for the cause. It is, we believe, a good rule for all crematories to follow; for a natural and praiseworthy interest is felt in new inventions, and we are apt to distrust them when they are veiled in mystery, and their details are not free for us to examine and to understand.

From year to year all the crematories that we have heard from show a steady and gratifying increase in the number of incinerations. We present the following table showing the number of incinerations that have taken place at the Fresh Pond Crematory since the first one, which occurred on December 4, 1885.

Number of incinerations for December, 1885. 9

" " . " " the year 1886. 77

" " " " " " 1887 67

" " " " " " 1888. 83

" " " " " " 1889. 106

" " " " " " 1890. 160

" " " " " " 1891. 187

" " " " Jan., Feb.,
and Mch., 1892. 56

Total number of incinerations from December
4, 1885, to April 1, 1892,. 745*

The birthplaces of these 745 persons are given in the annexed list:

Germany	373	Scotland	4
United States	240	Belgium	8
England	29	Holland	8
Austria	19	India	8
Switzerland	19	Cuba	2
France	16	Australia	1
Ireland	8	West Indies	1
Italy	7	Asia Minor	1
Hungary	8	Canada	1
Denmark	5	On Mediterranean	1

Unknown 1.

* "We give in the following table a comparison of the number of incinerations for the first five years, December to December, after the opening of the respective crematories :

" GOTHA.		NEW YORK.	
1878 to 1879.	16	1885 to 1886.	82
1879 " 1880.	17	1886 " 1887.	61
1880 " 1881.	34	1887 " 1888.	86
1881 " 1882	33	1888 " 1889.	108
1882 " 1883.	43	1889 " 1890.	152 "

—From *The Urn* of February, 1892.

They are classified as follows :

Men 468	Women . . . 213
Boys . . . 40	Girls 24

On the roll of those who have sought by means of fire to escape the corruption of the grave are the names of men well known and honored in their respective callings. Many were representatives of the learned professions, and the influence of such examples is undoubted. The occupations of some who have been incinerated at Fresh Pond, Long Island, is shown by the following list. Among the number were :

34 Merchants	6 Professors
28 Physicians	6 Of Dramatic Profession
17 Journalists	5 Druggists
15 Brokers	4 Scientific Engineers
12 Artists	4 Chemists
7 Teachers	2 Authors
	2 Clergymen.

The tables given above show that a belief in cremation is generally diffused, and that it is not confined to any one country or any especial calling. When we remember that throughout Europe and America to-day, the cause of cremation finds champions in thousands of educated men, who from character and position mould public opinion, we need not have any fear as to its future success. As Sir T. Spencer Wells said in his introduction to Dr. Erichsen's work: "When the people know how great are the evils dependent on burial in the earth, even when this is done under the most favorable conditions, how seldom these conditions can be secured, and, when the knowledge becomes general that when a human body which would require five, ten or twenty years to slowly putrefy in any soil can in one hour be cheaply and inoffensively converted into a white ash, public sentiment must favor cremation in place of corruption, and for putrefaction substitute purification."

That in time this system will be universally adopted, there seems no reason to doubt. We have faith in a good custom ultimately supplanting a bad one, and the superiority of incineration over earth-burial is manifest.

When the merits of the question are thoroughly appreciated, we shall not feel

justified in storing up disease-germs, and in
poisoning earth, air, and water by our present custom of burying the dead. We will
believe it neither wise nor decent to consign yearly to putrefaction within the
neighborhood of New York and Brooklyn
over 60,000 dead bodies. A refined sentiment will teach us the questionable nature
of that respect which prompts the erection
of a costly marble tribute to the memory
of a friend, while his body is left to decompose in a water-soaked grave beneath it.

　And, touching the religious aspect of the
case, if " religion," as asserted by Dr. Young,
" is the proof of common sense," then " let
us," in the words of the Rev. Howard
Henderson, " cease to count the beads of
our rosary, to chatter the litanies of prejudice, and address ourselves to the prob-
lems that philanthropy and piety present
to reason." " Let science and sanitation,"
says this reverend gentleman, " speak, and
give sentiment freedom. Treat the subject
fairly. It will not down at the bidding of
prejudice, nor be whistled down the wind
by a sniff of holy horror. The growth of

population is forcing the discussion upon
the thoughtful in all populous centres. It
is more a question of concern for the living
and the lowly, than for the dead. It must
not be studied amid the verdant shades and
sculptured tombs of Greenwood alone, but
amid the crowded cemeteries where the
poor and friendless are ditched and deserted."

Science and proven facts attest the wisdom of cremation, and in the words of the
Royal Institute of Science and Letters of
Lombardy, we believe that its adoption will
mark a stage of progress in the march of
civilization.

APPENDIX.

In the year 1889 the officers of the United States Cremation Co. (Limited), and the New York Cremation Society, forwarded to persons prominent in their respective callings, a circular-letter, asking for an expression of their views on the subject of cremation, as a means of furthering its introduction. A pamphlet of fifty-five pages, containing one hundred replies to this letter, was subsequently published for distribution.

The answers received, with but three or four exceptions, heartily endorsed the reform; and from about one third of these letters the following extracts are taken.

The Right Rev. Phillips Brooks, P. E. Bishop of Massachusetts, wrote:

"I believe that there are no true objections to the practice of cremation, and a good many excellent reasons why it should become common."

Charles A. Dana, Editor of *The Sun*, New York City :

"It is my judgment that cremation is the most rational and appropriate manner of disposing of the dead."

William A. Hammond, M.D., of the Sanitarium for Diseases of the Nervous System, Washington, D. C. :

"I have for many years past been heartily in favor of the cremation of the dead. So far as I can influence the matter I shall be cremated myself at the proper time."

Prof. Charles Eliot Norton, of Harvard University :

"The arguments in support of cremation are so strong, and those against our present fashion of burial are so conclusive, that I have little question that, when they are fairly presented to intelligent men, the development of a sentiment favorable to cremation will be rapid, and the adoption of the practice speedily become familiar."

The Hon. Abram S. Hewitt, New York :

"Eliminating the question of sentiment, which depends largely upon custom, it seems to me that cremation is the only sensible mode of disposing of the dead. I can imagine no argument against it, while all the considerations of public health are in its favor."

The Rev. R. Heber Newton, D.D., New York:

"I am glad of an opportunity of expressing my interest in the work of the Cremation Society. For many years I have thoroughly believed in cremation on a variety of grounds. Having tried to make my life one of usefulness to my fellows, I object to the possibility of injuring any one after I am dead. The thought that what I cannot take away with me to a higher form of life is to be left as a means of poisoning life is abhorrent to me. I prefer that my body shall be so disposed of as to put this out of the question. The religious objection has always been nonsensical to my mind. Believing thoroughly in a life to come, I have not the slightest notion of that higher life being conditioned in any possible way by the way in which we get into it. Nothing but the stupid prejudice of a blind orthodoxy, could allow any notion of this kind to have weight. In so far as it does have weight, it ought to be exposed and ridiculed. I have also, for years, had the intensest horror of thinking of any one dear to me undergoing the noxious process of decomposition, as we have made sure that it shall be made noxious by our whole mode of interment. I want those I love to pass from this life to a higher life without any such abhorrent decomposition of the form once dear to me.

"On every hand cremation has commended itself to my judgment, and I am sure that it is destined to prevail in the future. I expect to be disposed of thus myself, and do not know of any expression of opinion which I could offer that would have more weight than this."

Andrew Carnegie, New York:

"Cremation must be ranked as one of the greatest hygienic improvements of a progressive age. Its universal adoption is most desirable, and it is to be hoped that the people of this country—always heretofore quick to be educated in matters of reform—will soon recognize that cremation is something with which religious prejudice or false sentiment should not be allowed to interfere any more than with the other sanitary expedients of modern life. I am convinced that the adoption of cremation in preference to burial, in all the enlightened communities of this and other progressive countries, is only a question of time. Personally, of course, I am heartily in favor of it."

The Right Rev. Henry C. Potter, P. E. Bishop of New York :

" In reply to your inquiry, I beg to say that I have no prejudice unfavorable to cremation, and indeed in view of the curiously inadequate and singularly unintelligent arguments, attacks and denunciations which have been employed by those who are hostile to it, I have been rather disposed to sympathize with those who are seeking to introduce it."

Mrs. J. C. Croly (" Jennie June "), New York.

" I am heartily in sympathy with the Cremation Society, considering such disposition of human remains as the wisest, cleanest, most healthful and economical method of disposing of what is no longer of any use, and must in time become a positive source of injury."

The Hon. George Hoadly, Ex-Governor of Ohio :

" I thoroughly believe in cremation ; it is the most wholesome and best method of disposing of the dead. I should prefer for myself and those I love, if cremation were common, to adopt it, rather than to leave the body to moulder in the ground and be the prey of worms."

Clement Cleveland, M.D., New York:

"I am heartily in favor of the reform you are advocating. The sanitary consideration is the one that chiefly influences me, and to my mind is of such vital importance that it outweighs all conceivable objections."

James Lewis Howe, M.D., P.H.D., Louisville, Ky. :

"I do not believe there is a single argument against cremation which is worthy the name of argument."

Charles Francis Adams, Boston :

"I have never been able to understand any of the arguments against cremation. The religious argument certainly has no bearing on the subject.

"As a matter of sentiment, I fail to see why we should rather consign the remains of those we love to the tender mercies of worms than to the tender mercies of heat.

"The sanitary argument is, of course, all in favor of cremation. By burying the bodies of the dead in the ground, we preserve, in so far as we can, and spread, germs of disease. Under these circumstances, I am unable to see what the modern system of burying corpses in the soil has to rest upon, except custom and that prejudice which springs from custom."

The Rev. John L. Scudder, Pastor of the
First Congregational Church, Jersey City :

" I believe in cremation with all my heart,
and consider it the only proper method of disposing of the dead. The arguments in its favor
are overwhelming. I am glad to see that prejudice and blind conservatism are rapidly giving
way to nineteenth-century common-sense. I
prophesy that inside of twenty-five years cremation will become well-nigh universal in this
country. Advancing civilization demands it
and will have it. My own sister was cremated
at Fresh Pond, and my father, Rev. Henry M.
Scudder, D.D., for so many years pastor of the
Central Congregational Church, New York, has
left orders to the effect that, upon his decease,
his body shall be brought to this country from
Japan, where he is now residing, and cremated
in the State of New York. It is also my desire
and command that when I die my body shall
be disposed of in a similar manner. I prefer a
' fiery chariot ' to being eaten up by worms."

Mrs. Lippincott (" Grace Greenwood ") :

" I have given a great deal of serious thought
to the subject of cremation, and heartily en-
dorse all movements in that direction. The
world, even the Christian world, must come to
it finally—though it denounce it now ever

so sternly as 'a heathen custom.' The world
must come to it, or see the above-ground living
poisoned by their under-ground dead. For
economic as well as sanitary reasons I would
advocate cremation. I saw much of the working of the system at Milan ; saw that it took a
great burden of care and expense from poor
families, bereaved and left in straitened circumstances. Surely it is the simplest, the
surest and purest manner of rendering 'ashes
to ashes'—of giving back our mortal part to
the immortal elements."

Professor Felix Adler, New York :

" My views on the subject of cremation are
entirely in accord with your own. I believe
that this method of disposing of the remains of
those who were dear to us in life is more reverent, more in harmony with refined feelings,
besides being obviously superior on grounds of
public health, to the usual practice of earth-
burial. I trust that, thanks to your efforts and
those of your coadjutors, cremation will be
received with increasing favor by all enlightened persons in the community."

The Rev. D. S. Rainsford, D.D., Rector of
St. George's Church, New York :

" You may quote me as heartily favoring the
objects of your Company."

Charles A. Bacon, M.D., Washington, D. C.:
" The sanitary necessities of civilized life
render this reform inevitable—an affair of time
only. Cremation must be adopted by all civilized communities as a preventive to disease,
and the day when this shall be the adopted
method of disposing of the remains of our dead,
is not far distant."

Col. Thomas W. Knox, New York:

" I am heartily in favor of cremation, and
have directed in my will that my body shall be
cremated, and the ashes placed at the disposal
of my nearest relatives and friends.

" The Cremation Company and the Cremation Society have done excellent work, and are
to be warmly commended for their long and
earnest battle against prejudice in its various
forms."

Kate Field, Washington, D. C.:

" I am a cremationist because earth-burial
poisons earth, air and water, and consequently
breeds disease among the living. . . . Cremation is not only the healthiest and cleanest
but the most poetical way of disposing of the
dead. Whoever prefers loathsome worms to
ashes possesses a strange imagination."

The Hon. Charles W. Horner, Washington, D. C. :

" I have so far acted on the opinion, now rapidly becoming universal, that cremation is the best way for the disposal of dead bodies, as to make it one of the clauses of my last will."

The Rev. Edward Everett Hale, D.D., Boston :

" I have no doubt that cremation will work its way into general favor, and I am glad to think so. I am glad to remember that in *Old and New*, now more than fourteen years ago, I published a well-considered article urging the reform in burial."

Robert P. Porter, Editor of *The Press*, New York :

" In reply to your letter asking my opinion in relation to the advantages of cremation as a means of disposing of the dead, I beg leave to say that I am heartily in favor of it, and that I look forward to the day when it will be universally adopted by civilized nations."

Moncure D. Conway, New York :

" I regard the wholesale poisoning of the earth and its fountains by dead bodies as the survival of a grossly materialistic conception of the future life. Surely our New World civilization should replace the loathsome vault with the pure urn."

Lucy Stone, of the American Woman Suffrage Association, Boston :

" I am decidedly in favor of cremation. On sanitary grounds alone it seems to me to be wholly desirable."

Edgar Fawcett, New York :

" I am a believer in cremation. I feel 'convinced that it is one of those reforms which will some day be universally adopted."

Rose Elizabeth Cleveland :

" I am very willing to say that I have long felt that by cremation the body after death is returned most properly to its predestined ashes. On the theory I am very clear, and in my own case I should desire that cremation should take place."

The Rev. William Hayes Ward, D.D., Editor of *The Independent :*

" I am aware of no argument against cremation that deserves consideration, and I regard that method of disposing of the bodies of the dead as intelligent reason and unperverted taste."

Henry Tuck, M.D., Vice-President of " The New York Life Insurance Co." :

" I am glad of the opportunity of again expressing my hearty approval of the practice of cremation."

Ella Wheeler Wilcox :

" I heartily approve of cremation. In the first place, it is cleanly ; in the second place, it is economical. It helps along nature. The body must eventually turn to dust, and why not turn it to dust by cremation rather than have it decompose in the ground. Then, again, the increase in population and, consequently, death, must render this mode of disposing of the dead eventually necessary. I cannot see why the old Greek custom was ever done away with."

The Rev. John W. Chadwick, Brooklyn :

" I do not think I can do better than refer you to an article in *The Forum* (No. 3, if I remember rightly) for my very favorable opinion of cremation, which I am not likely to change to a less favorable opinion at any time."

William Waldorf Astor, New York:

" You ask my opinion of cremation. I think the opposition to it has largely originated in an ignorant prejudice. The objections raised against it have certainly lost much of their force in public estimation. Sanitary considerations are strongly in its favor, and, as concerns sentimental feelings, it seems to me there is much to recommend a total and immediate destruction of the body after death."

Edgar Saltus, New York:

" I am an enthusiastic believer in cremation."

Lillie Devereux Blake, New York:

" You may use my name as that of an advocate of cremation, as I certainly think it the most desirable method of disposing of the bodies of our dead."

Marshall P. Wilder, New York:

" I am unable to see any valid objection to cremation, and to my mind it seems to be in consonance with the spirit of the age."

The Rev. Theodore C. Williams, New York:

" I believe that merely on grounds of feeling, the considerations of decent respect due to the remains of the dead are increasingly in favor of cremation. The grave, the tomb, are necessarily revolting to any imagination that looks beyond the surface. Cremation, on the contrary, can suggest none but pure and elevated conceptions. I find large numbers of persons, especially young people, who express a desire for this reform."

The late Samuel L. M. Barlow, New York :

" Apart from the question of sentiment merely, it seems to me that there is but one rational method of disposing of our dead, and that is by cremation. When this question is understood, all the objections to it that I have heard will vanish, and we shall through cremation avoid all the repulsive features which are inseparable from all present forms of earth-burial, and, what is of more consequence, the dangers to the general public health which attend the present system."

Henry M. Taber, New York :

" I have carefully considered the subject for many years, and am well satisfied of the advantages afforded by cremation over burial. The· sanitary reason alone ought to have sufficient weight to override every objection that can be offered, and will in time *demand* its general adoption in the interest of the living (if for no other reason)."

Mme. Alice D. Le Plongeon, Brooklyn :

"I am most decidedly in favor of burning the dead, and cannot comprehend why so many object to it. The terrible diseases that from time to time cast communities of human beings into an abyss of grief, would lose their hold in a short time if the victims were promptly consigned to the purifying action of the flames. What possible good can there be in burning clothes and furniture, if the infected flesh be allowed to remain in existence. In 1868 there was a dreadful epidemic of yellow fever in Lima, Peru ; as many as three hundred patients dying each day. From the beginning, Dr. Le Plongeon, then practicing in that city, urged the cremation of the dead. It was impossible to bring the public mind to contemplate such a course. Finally an arrangement was made to keep large fires on the trenches filled with corpses, public attention not being drawn to the fact. At once the plague abated and soon died out.

"Do mourners ever reflect what a disgusting sight would meet their gaze if the flower-laden sod was lifted from the remains of their beloved ones? The thought is terrible! To my mind, rapid incineration rids death of half its horror. The sacred frame that has been so long inhabited by the dear friend is wafted to the pure element, instead of being trod beneath the feet of coming generations. Often and often have we seen in ancient deserted cities, skulls kicked about like balls (by unthinking fools to whom nothing is sacred), and the sight has aroused a thousand thoughts. . . . Unless the ocean waves engulf me, I trust that some friend will kindly see my remains confided to the fiery furnace."

The Rev. J. E. Raymond, New York:

" Any objection to the practice of cremation must be founded either upon ignorance, superstition, or sentiment. The enlightened Christian conscience must approve it. It is one of those great reforms which are possible only in an age of scientific progress, and which make their way in spite of bigotry and conservatism. When prejudice and fanaticism are overcome, the adoption of cremation will be almost universal. It is only a matter of time."

Views of " Shirley Dare," from *The Epoch* of November 23, 1888:

" From the first mention of cremation, I have had but one opinion, that it is the only safe, Christian, becoming way of disposing of the dead. Fifteen years ago I wrote directions to have my own body cremated at last, and the only horror death holds for me is that the wish may by any chance be unfulfilled. How can we leave our friendless dead to the slow changes and deformity of the grave? How can we bear to poison earth and air by reminders of what was dearest on earth to us? The most fearful and heathenish of all the mockeries which deface this half-civilized age of the world are its burials, in which we leave our beloved to a fate impossible to think of. No wonder the words ' grave ' and ' hell ' are interchangeable in Scripture."

Views of Frances E. Willard, as expressed in her *Glimpses of Fifty Years.*

" I have the purpose to help forward progressive movements, even in my latest hours, and hence hereby decree that the earthly mantle which I shall drop ere long, when my real self passes onward into the world unseen, shall be swiftly enfolded in flames and rendered powerless harmfully to affect the health of the living. Let no friend of mine say aught to prevent the cremation of my cast-off body. The fact that the popular mind has not come to this decision renders it all the more my duty, who have seen the light, to stand for it in death, as I have sincerely meant in life to stand by the great cause of poor, oppressed humanity."

REGULATIONS

OF THE UNITED STATES CREMATION COMPANY (LIMITED) GOVERNING INCINERATION.

I. Applications for incineration must be made at the office of the Company, No. 62 East Houston Street, New York City.

II. Each application must be made by the person having charge of the disposal of the body, or his representative ; a blank form prepared by the Company must be filled out and filed in the office of the Company.

III. On the filling out of said application blank, payment of the incineration fee, and presentation of the Physician's Certificate stating time, place, and cause of death, an order directing the incineration will be given the applicant ; to this order the undertaker in charge of the body must have attached the customary certificate of the Board of Health, and such other permits as may be prerequisite to a lawful interment in the State of New York and the township and county where the Crematory is located.

Upon the arrival at the appointed hour of the remains at the Crematory, this order, with the said certificate and permits attached, must be delivered to the Superintendent. This rule is imperative, and unless the order is accompanied by the necessary certificate and permits in due form, the incineration will not be allowed to take place.

IV. Every incineration shall be attended by some relative of the deceased or representative of the family.

V. The price of incineration is $35, always payable in advance.

VI. The body may be conveyed to the Crematory in such a manner as the friends of the deceased may select; where desired the Company will convey the body to the Crematory, at an expense not exceeding the usual charge for like service.

VII. No special preparation of the body or clothing is necessary. The body is always incinerated in the clothing as received.

VIII. It is expected that the funeral services will terminate prior to the removal of the body to the Crematory; but where desired, ceremonies or services may be held at the Crematory in connection with the incineration, without any extra charge.

IX. The coffin in which the body is carried to the Crematory is never allowed to be removed from the building, but is burned after the incineration.

X. In every instance of death from contagious disease the ·coffin will be burned with the body, and no exposure of the body will be permitted.

XI. Incineration may be as private as the friends of the deceased desire. On the day following the incineration the ashes will be deliverable at the office of the Company, in a receptacle provided by it free of cost.

XII. On one day's notice bodies coming from a distance will, on their arrival in New York or Jersey City, be received by the Company's undertaker, who will procure, where the relatives desire it, the necessary permits and take complete charge of all arrangements.

Further information can be obtained on application personally or by letter at the Company's office in New York City.

www.ingramcontent.com/pod-product-compliance
Lightning Source LLC
Chambersburg PA
CBHW030606040726
47497CB00008B/2866